THE GIRL BEHIND THE GLASS

Also by Jane Kelley
Nature Girl

THE GIRL BEHIND THE GLASS

Jane Kelley

A YEARLING BOOK

Text copyright © 2011 by Jane Kelley
Cover art copyright © 2011 by Jaime Zollars

All rights reserved. Published in the United States by Yearling, an imprint of Random House Children's Books, a division of Random House, Inc., New York. Originally published in hardcover in the United States by Random House Children's Books, New York, in 2011.

Yearling and the jumping horse design are registered trademarks of Random House, Inc.

Visit us on the Web!
randomhouse.com/kids

Educators and librarians, for a variety of teaching tools, visit us at randomhouse.com/teachers

The Library of Congress has cataloged the hardcover edition of this work as follows:
Kelley, Jane (Jane Alice)
The girl behind the glass / Jane Kelley. — 1st ed.
p. cm.
Summary: Moving from Brooklyn to a rental house in the country strains the relationship between eleven-year-old identical twins Hannah and Anna Zimmer, a situation made worse by the ghost of a girl who is trapped in the house because of problems with her own sister eighty years before.
ISBN 978-0-375-86220-5 (trade) — ISBN 978-0-375-96220-2 (lib. bdg.) — ISBN 978-0-375-86219-9 (pbk.) — ISBN 978-0-375-88996-7 (ebook)
[1. Sisters—Fiction. 2. Twins—Fiction. 3. Moving, Household—Fiction. 4. Ghosts—Fiction. 5. Family life—Fiction.] I. Title.
PZ7.K28168Gir 2011 [Fic]—dc22 2010043568

Printed in the United States of America

10 9 8 7 6 5 4 3 2 1

First Yearling Edition 2012

For my mother, Virginia Carson Kelley,
who inspired me with her love of books—
and the Bastable children

The night is darkening round me,
The wild winds coldly blow;
But a tyrant spell has bound me
And I cannot, cannot go.
—Emily Brontë, "Spellbound"

"Girls!"

No one had said that word in the house on Hemlock Road in an awfully long time.

"GIRLS!"

A woman stood on the front porch behind a curtain of rain, calling out to somebody. Could she be talking to actual girls?

There hadn't been any humans living in the house for over a year. Oh, people drove by to stare. Boys threw their rocks at Halloween. A few ran all the way up to the front porch and boasted they were brave. Sometimes in the spring, when it wasn't so gloomy, people considered moving in. Men tramped through the rooms and asked about the electrical wiring. Women hoped to find charming details under the peeling paint. There was a fancy hall tree mirror by the front door. For some reason, no one liked to see their reflection in that cracked glass.

Then, just as summer was ending and the chokeberry bush by the front porch was tinged with red, a man hurried through the rooms. He didn't even look in the attic or the basement. Soon after that, workers replaced the broken windows and swept up the trash. Painters covered the gray walls with white. Furniture was dragged in. The front hall filled with boxes. Only the lazy mice were glad—humans made it so much easier for them to find food. The spiders hated having their webs swept away. After all these years, the bats and some others just wanted to be left alone.

And yet everything could be different if girls were in the house.

"Come unpack!"

There hadn't been any yelling in the house either. There had been screaming. And shrieking. And gasping. And that odd, strangulated flutter from the back of that old man's throat. But there hadn't been any yelling like only mothers could do.

The woman had bright orange hair, cut so short it stood up. Her earrings were feathers and bits of cloth. She wore denim trousers, like everybody always did these days. Her shirt had been pieced together in odd and colorful ways. She didn't look at all like a mother. But she was. She was so angry; it was easy to know her thoughts. She was thinking how much work she had to do before her family could sleep in the house that night. She was thinking those girls were plenty old enough to help. She was thinking she hoped it wasn't a mistake to move to this house on Hemlock Road.

"Stop hiding in the car!"

A silver car was parked in the driveway, not far from the hemlock trees. Rain rattled on its roof. The fogged windows made it difficult to see in or out. But there they were, two girls sitting side by side on the backseat.

The girls both had long noses and straight brown hair, cut just above their shoulders. They were identical twins. That was the most wonderful way to have a sister. No one could be jealous of the other when they both had very green eyes.

They wore denim shorts and shirts with red words. The blue shirt had a drawing of a pigeon and the words PARK SLOPE. The orange shirt had a drawing of a squirrel and the words PARK SLOPE. The girls looked like they were eleven—the most perfect age for them to be.

"Hannah Anna, I'm losing my patience with you!"

One twin was thinking that she didn't recognize that yelling woman. Someone must have put an evil spell on their mom.

The other twin was wishing she had paid attention to the roads. Then she could drive them back to Brooklyn.

Which one was Hannah? Which one was Anna? Knowing their minds didn't help. Most people never said their names with their thoughts.

Their heads were bent over a notebook. Each twin made a different part of the same picture. They were good at drawing. Their straight lines were very straight. The girls knew what to make big and what to keep little. They were making a city street shaded by tall trees. The buildings on the side were all crammed together. Nine steps led up to the front doors, past tiny yards full of flowers. At the end of the street, you could see a café with tables where people sipped drinks from mugs. Next to it was a bookstore. One twin was drawing it. The other was drawing two girls hurrying toward the store.

Of course they were hurrying. It looked like the kind of place that anybody who loved to read would long to visit. But no one could go there. It was just a picture.

The twins thought that too. It was just a picture.

They both looked up at the house on Hemlock Road.

The house always looked gloomier when it rained. The brick walls, the shrubs, the chimney, and the roof were all very gray. Once upon a time, the walls were white. The trim around the windows was bright green. The shutters didn't sag. Red geraniums blossomed in the window boxes. The chokeberry bush was trimmed back from the porch so there was room for a wooden bench. The hemlock trees were only half as tall, so it didn't seem like the sun never shined. Once upon a time, the house on Hemlock Road had been somebody's home. It wasn't anymore. But maybe, just maybe, it could be now.

The girls went back to their drawing. One added a book to the display in the shopwindow. The other drew a purse so they could bring money to the store.

But they already had books. There were six boxes labeled BOOKS in the hall and more upstairs by the bedrooms. The girls could open those boxes, take out those books, and read whichever ones they wanted to. Hadn't their mother told the girls to go inside? Other mothers would get very angry if they weren't obeyed. So why didn't this mother make the twins unpack their books?

Maybe they actually had a copy of the best book in the world, about the funniest, most adventuresome children ever. Even if they didn't have *The Story of the Treasure Seekers*, there must be some good books in all those boxes. What if there weren't? What if all their books were like the two in the canvas bag by their feet? *The Golden Compass* and *The Subtle Knife*. What kind of girl would want to read a book about nautical history or whetstones?

"I miss our bookstore."

"Our street."

"Our tree."

"Our squirrel."

"Nutkin."

The twins spoke quickly. They hardly needed any words to understand each other. They knew what they were thinking. They were almost as clever at reading minds as some others were. Sadly, though, the twins only understood each other.

Everybody in the car sighed a deep and painful sigh.

"But we had to move."

"Because of Selena."

Who was that?

Then, as if she had actually heard that question, one twin pointed to the second-story window on the south side of the house.

An older girl was waving at the car. She had long golden hair. It was shocking to see her there. It shouldn't have been. Lots of teenage girls had hair like that. They used it as a curtain to hide their treachery.

"She picked."

"Who cares what room we get?"

"It won't be Brooklyn."

They should care. The bedroom where Selena pranced was the second biggest. The parents would have chosen the biggest bedroom, on the south side. Nearly all the people who had lived in the house had slept there, except for that old man who made the mistake of wanting to be closer to the bathroom. The third bedroom in the back was the smallest. It had the worst possible view of the worst possible place. Why should the twins have to sleep there? Why should Selena get the second-best bedroom? Only an accident of birth made her the oldest and gave her all that yellow hair.

"Hannah Anna! Why are you still in the car?"

Now a man stood on the front porch. He must have been the father, even though his brown hair curled over the back of his neck. He was wearing a faded shirt with the words PINK FLOYD THE WALL by a picture of a colorful swirl. He was thinking that this was the second-worst day of his life. He thought about the worst day too. Since it was something that had happened at his office, reading those thoughts wasn't worth the bother.

He tried to be cheerful. "Selena has some great ideas for how you can decorate your bedroom."

"Oh wow," one twin said.

"Selena had an idea," the other twin said.

The father frowned. "You aren't even trying to make the best of this situation."

The twins didn't answer. They both thought there was no best to this situation.

"I'll give you one minute."

And then what? Was he the kind of father who would tell his daughters to go cut a switch from the chokeberry bush?

"Please, Anna?" he said.

"We want to finish our drawing," said the twin who must have been Anna.

"Come on inside, Hannah. Selena will think you're mad at her," the father said.

Hannah thought that for a change Selena would be right.

"I'll tell her you're on your way." The father went back inside the house. The door blew shut behind him and bumped his rear end. Ha!

Unfortunately the twins didn't notice that little prank. They kept drawing. Hannah made a plate of cookies on the café table. Then Anna put a cat in the door of the bookstore.

Cats were not welcome here.

One branch of the hemlock tree waved furiously.

Although the twins understood each other, they didn't understand the wind. They didn't see the branch. They didn't even look up from the page.

Why wouldn't they go in? The house wouldn't be so bad. They had their books. They had each other. Some of the critters were friendly.

Go in.

Were they afraid? They didn't need to be, if they stayed away from certain spots. Avoided the potent places where things had happened—or things had not happened. As long as the twins did that, nothing would harm them. Really and truly, the house was not as bad as . . .

Suddenly there was a loud scream.

❧ 2 ❧

"EEEEEEEEK!"

No scream is as shrill as the scream of a teenage girl. No scream is as loud or as long. This scream lasted the entire time that Selena ran out of the second-best bedroom and down the stairs.

Everybody else ran too. The mice scuttled to safety under the floorboards. The mother and the father rushed out of the kitchen. And Hannah and Anna finally left the car and hurried inside the house.

The family stood in the front hall next to the hall tree mirror, panting with excitement.

"What happened?" the father said.

What had happened to make Selena's face so red and her blue eyes so wide?

"I was upstairs, in my new closet," she said.

She had gone in the closet? Even the mice knew

better than to do that. But she had waltzed right in. Her clothes were all she cared about. That was obvious from how perfectly the stripes on her shirt matched the stitching on her short shorts and the color on her toenails. She was just like other teenage girls who never paid attention to anything that really mattered.

"What happened?" the mother said.

Selena searched for words. But she wouldn't find them.

"Did you see a mouse?" The mother thought about the teeth marks she had seen on some of the boxes.

"Or a spider?" Anna said.

"How about a teensy bug?" Hannah said.

"Don't tease her. Can't you see she's upset?" Of course the mother took the older sister's side. She even smoothed that long yellow hair. "Just tell us what happened, Selena."

Now Selena had a new fear—that she would sound stupid. She shrugged. "It was nothing, really. Just a weird feeling, you know?"

Did they know? Could they know?

"A feeling like maybe . . . ," Hannah said.

"We shouldn't have moved here?" Anna said.

"No!" Selena said.

"You all know perfectly well we can't move into our new house yet because it isn't ready," the mother said.

"You can't live in a house that doesn't have a toilet," the father said.

Selena thought she would have preferred that.

"Come on, let's go look," the father said.

No one moved.

"Back in the closet?" Selena's voice squeaked.

"I'm sure there's nothing there," the father said.

They all looked up along the dark curved banister and held their breath to listen.

They hoped to hear nothing. But not even death is silent. There are always noises everywhere—especially in the house on Hemlock Road. Sure enough, something skittered across the floor upstairs. It wasn't a feeling—it was a mouse who had been chewing on a box and decided to make a break for a better hiding place. Only the family didn't know that.

The twins grabbed each other. Selena grabbed herself. The mother grabbed the father. The father grabbed the nearest object that seemed most like a weapon. Nobody in the family laughed as he held up the toilet plunger.

A parade went up the stairs. Plunger, father, mother, twins, and Selena bringing up the rear. The father stomped his feet. He thought that if he made enough noise, he would scare away whatever was in the closet. That might have been true—if it was a living thing.

At the top of the stairs, he walked along the landing toward the right. He pushed open the door to the second-best bedroom with the wooden end of the plunger. The family peeped inside. What did they expect to see? A burglar? A bum? Or maybe, as another mother used to say, a green-eyed monster was in the room.

"Nothing," the father said.

He walked more bravely now, around a bed with a white headboard, a white bureau, a white desk, and three tall boxes each labeled WARDROBE. There were other boxes too. None of them were labeled BOOKS.

Selena pointed to the back of the room, where the closet door was still partially ajar. The father tiptoed over to it. He used the wooden end to pry it open. He quickly retreated, as if he expected something to jump out at him and say, *Boo!*

Nothing did. There was nothing in the closet. Nothing that could be seen. But now that the door was opened wide for the first time in years, a smell escaped into the bedroom.

The twins didn't notice. They had spotted something else—an opportunity to tease Selena. If she was as cruel as most older sisters, she deserved it.

Anna nudged Hannah. "Look there."

"Oh no, it can't be," Hannah said.

"Yes, it is," Anna said.

"The terrible," Hannah said.

"Terrifying," Anna said.

"Dreadful," Hannah said.

"Void," Anna and Hannah said together.

"Ha-ha," Selena said.

Nothing about the void was funny.

The mother wrinkled her nose. "Do you smell that?"

The father sniffed and leaned back. "The closet *is* next to the bathroom."

"The monster that scared Selena didn't flush," Anna said.

The twins raced each other out of the bedroom and into the bathroom. Although the water whooshed down the pipe, it didn't carry away the smell. Or the memory of what had happened in the closet. Nothing could. Nothing would. It was best not to go where that foul anger still lived.

Slowly the closet door shut.

"It must have been the wind," the father said.

His family believed him—at least for now.

Before the twins could escape to the car, their mother put her arms around them and pushed them down the hall past the bathroom, to the left and into their bedroom.

It was, as has been said, the smallest, darkest, worst bedroom. It hadn't always seemed so. Once upon a time, the wall without windows had a bookcase with two shelves of books and a collection of three little china birds. There had been four until a mean, fluffy orange cat knocked off the robin and smashed it. A blue chair used to be in front of the shelves, just in case someone wanted to grab a different book to read.

Of course those books had been confiscated a long time ago. For no good reason! A few days after that, everything else in the room had been taken away. Nobody cared much about the curtains. Nobody needed the chair or the bed. But losing the books was cruel and horrible. The characters in those pages had been better than friends.

Better not get upset again. Better not let anger burn. Once the fire started, everything got black like smoke. Even the things that had been nice. Better not think about the future or the past. Just be like the other critters. Just be.

Only for almost eighty years, there hadn't been *any* good books in the house on Hemlock Road. Some people had brought boring ones, like encyclopedias or almanacs or *Basic Cooking*. Many clung to their Bibles, especially at night. One man hadn't had any books at all—just magazines full of nasty pictures. Fortunately the mice soon chewed those all up.

And now girls had come. The room was full of marvelous things again. A bunk bed, a red bookcase with six shelves, a double desk, two yellow chairs, and three big cardboard boxes labeled H/A BOOKS. Someone had already cut the tape. It didn't take much of a breeze to blow the flap open. A little more air made it waggle back and forth temptingly.

The twins stood side by side looking at the yard. Without curtains, the windows stared out back with unblinking eyes.

What did the girls see? Nothing very interesting. A ditch. That was all. The ditch was empty now. Nobody was pacing back and forth. So why did they keep staring at it? They had books to read. Books could carry them away. Didn't they want that? Didn't they need that? Maybe not. They had each other. They hadn't been left alone with nothing.

The cardboard slapped against the side of the box of books again and again.

The twins moved a little closer to each other.

"That's weird," Hannah said.

"Just a draft." Anna went to close the window. It wasn't open.

They looked at each other and wondered.

Their mother called, "Hannah Anna! Your dad went out and got dinner!"

The twins ran down the steps and passed the hall tree mirror without looking in the glass.

"What did you get?"

"Indian?"

"Sushi?"

"Middle Eastern?"

They gasped when they saw the yellow-and-white bag their father held up.

"Oh no."

"Not fast food."

"Are you trying to kill us?"

For one brief moment, their father thought he would like to. Instead he gave them each a small red cardboard container. The family all sat on boxes in the dining room to eat sandwiches and crispy potato strips. They drank from straws stuck into enormous paper cups like the ones that often ended up in the ditch next to Hemlock Road.

The family didn't talk much. They were all tired and yet they all wondered whether they would be able to sleep. The fast food was indeed eaten very quickly. Then dinner was over. The mother helpfully gathered up the uneaten bits and put them in a corner of the kitchen where the mice could easily find them.

"I'm going to bed," the mother said.

"Me too," the father said.

"Good night," the mother said.

"Sweet dreams," the father said.

As if saying that could make it so.

The parents climbed the stairs. Would Hannah and Anna go with them? No. Hannah got the canvas bag. Then finally, at long last, she and Anna took out their books.

In the living room, there was a long gray sofa covered with a sort of leather more suitable for shoes. The cushions leaned against the wall, still wrapped in plastic. The twins sat on the sofa anyway, with their backs propped against the sofa's arms. Their feet met in the middle. Hannah held *The Subtle Knife* and Anna held *The Golden Compass*.

The nautical adventure seemed more promising than the whetstone. And it was. *The Golden Compass* was actually about a clever girl named Lyra who was searching for her friend. Anna read quickly, skipping to her favorite parts. This was a shame because not everyone had read the book before. It was confusing. Could someone's best friend be a daemon? Maybe so.

Selena came in. "We could trade rooms, if you want. Except the ceiling is lower in my room so your bunk beds wouldn't fit. And I know you like sleeping on top of each other, don't you?"

The twins each turned a page in their books.

"Didn't you tell me once how you like to have the same dream floating above your heads? I thought that was the cutest thing. You always said cute things when you were little."

She waited, hoping they would move so she could sit. They didn't. They didn't want her anywhere near them.

"When will you be done reading?" Selena said.

What kind of a question was that? How could anyone ever be done reading?

The twins each turned another page.

"There's nothing for me to do," Selena said.

Hannah and Anna slammed shut their books.

"Whose fault is that?" Anna said.

"Dad should have hooked up the TV," Selena said.

Hannah and Anna looked at each other. They said nothing in a very loud way.

"It isn't *my* fault," Selena said.

"Hmmm," Anna said. "Why did we move here, Hannah?"

"Gee, Anna, I don't remember."

"You think you're so funny," Selena said.

"Maybe we got bored living in the most perfect neighborhood," Anna said.

"Rated in the top ten by the National Realtors Association."

"You're really annoying," Selena said.

~18~

"However, since we intend to be famous writers," Hannah said.

"Or politicians," Anna said.

"We shouldn't have perfect childhoods."

"We had to move to Helton."

"So we could suffer."

Selena covered her ears. Nothing could keep hurtful words from boring into a person's brain.

Some might have remembered other people's cruel words and felt sorry for Selena. But it was impossible to forget that teenagers were two-faced. One moment, they seemed nice. The next, they would blithely watch someone die.

"Don't forget Dad," Hannah said.

"He wanted a longer commute to Manhattan."

"He can edit lots of articles riding three hours on the train."

"Mom wanted to move," Selena said.

"Really?" Hannah and Anna said.

"She's glad to have a whole room for making her designs," Selena said.

"She has to say that," Anna said.

"So you won't feel like you ruined *all* our lives," Hannah said.

Selena snatched the books away from her sisters and threw them on the floor.

"Hey!" everybody said.

"You shouldn't be mad at me. I *tried* to get into a decent high school in New York City. I don't do good on tests."

"Don't do *well*," Hannah said.

"You're just not very smart," Anna said.

"I'm smart in other ways," Selena said.

"If you believe that, then you really are dumb," Hannah said.

Now that was a very mean thing to say—even if it was true.

Selena stormed out of the living room, past the hall tree mirror, and partway up the steps. When she could see above the landing and into her bedroom, she stopped.

The door to the bedroom was open. The dark oozed across the floor as if it were a thick kind of mud.

Hannah and Anna could have picked up their books and gone back to reading. Instead they watched Selena hesitate on the stairs. Then Anna got an idea. Hannah was good at reading minds. She knew what her twin sister was thinking. They slid off the sofa and quietly crept out of the living room into the front hall. When they were right beneath the stairway, they jumped up and shouted, "Boo!"

Selena screamed and ran into her parents' room. Unfortunately the father was undressing. She screamed again at the sight of his blue-striped undershorts and ran to the front hall.

The father put on his pajama bottoms and came out. "What's going on?"

"Hannah Anna are so mean," Selena said.

"Don't tease your sister," the mother came downstairs to say.

"We were only having fun," Anna said.

"However we can in this awful house," Hannah said.

"You're the awful ones," Selena said.

"Girls, please. Fighting makes everything worse. Everybody should go to bed," the mother said.

"I can't sleep. My heart's still pounding," Selena said.

"I hope so," Hannah said.

"Or you'd be dead," Anna said.

"Stop that kind of talk," the father said.

"Can I sleep in your room, Mom?" Selena said. "It isn't fair that I'm the only one who has to sleep all by herself."

How dare she talk about what was fair?

Once again the mother took the oldest daughter's side. "Sure you can."

The father even fetched her pillow and blankets so she wouldn't have to go into her bedroom to get them.

Hannah and Anna were left alone downstairs.

They got back in their spots on the sofa and opened their books. They hadn't read more than a few pages before Hannah said, "How long will Mom and Dad let her sleep with them?"

"I don't know."

"She really was scared."

"Did you see her?"

"When she screamed?"

They made their faces into grotesque masks.

Anna laughed, but Hannah wondered, "What do you think she felt in the closet?"

"Nothing," Anna said.

Hannah wasn't so sure. She remembered the way the door slowly shut.

"She's just being a teenager. They have way too many emotions," Anna said.

The twins also had too many emotions. None of them were good. They hated the house. They wanted to leave. So did everybody else. Everybody wanted to go far, far away from the house on Hemlock Road.

But leaving was impossible for some.

Anna smiled. She wasn't happy; she had another idea. "Mom and Dad would do anything for Selena."

Hannah smiled too. "So if Selena hates it here."

"Mom and Dad will leave."

"Since the new house isn't ready."

"We have to kick out the renters."

"And go home."

"To Brooklyn."

They slapped hands in triumph.

"We need to scare her," Hannah said.

"We need a plan," Anna said.

"A supernatural plan."

They left their books and took the notebook with their drawing upstairs. For the first time all day, they were happy. They felt confident about their scheme because they knew they were clever and they had each other.

But they would never get their lives back to what had been. Never never never. No matter how many years they tried.

When the humans were all in bed, the critters began to stir. The mice had a lovely feast on those bits of meat and rolls. Then they gnawed the boxes that smelled most promisingly of food. The spiders repaired their damaged webs. The best excitement was in the attic, when the bats unfurled their wings and let go of the rafters.

The bats swooped around the empty space. They paid no attention to the father's spluttering snores. For a few moments, all fifty bats moved together to make a great gray beast. Oh, it was swell to soar like that. Then it was over. One by one, the bats slipped through the gaps by the eaves and out into the night to kill.

Boundaries meant nothing to them. They went wherever they could find food. Some flew over the ditch. Some flew between the hemlocks and beyond the road. Others flew toward the nearest neighbor, who lived on the south side of the house—the revolting old woman who opened cans of food for the wild cats.

Tonight the cats hissed and fought. Then the yowling started. *Yrrow, yrrow, yrrow.* As if they were in torment. Why should they be in pain? They had plenty of food. They came and went, doing exactly what they pleased. They weren't stuck next to the last place on earth they would ever want to be. How could they suffer—they didn't care one bit about the living or the dead.

Yrrow, yrrow, yrrow. The sound drove the bats farther and farther away. Even the ones who usually hunted in the yard left. Then there was no reason to stay outside— especially when the house had so many interesting things in it now.

The twins' books were on the sofa. According to the cover, *The Subtle Knife* was a sequel to *The Golden Compass.* Because they were both facedown, they couldn't be read. There was no way to flip the pages. The twins had been very careless and inconsiderate. Other children never treated their books like that.

The father was still snoring. Selena made little sounds as she slept. Was she saying "me" or "mean"? Who cared about the parents or the older sister? The twins' dreams would be much more interesting. Almost like listening to a friend.

Hannah and Anna were sleeping next to each other on the bottom bunk. Hannah held a pencil. Anna held their notebook. They hadn't added to their picture of the Brooklyn street. They had turned to a new page. Along the top, one of them had written: *Ghost in Selena's closet?*

One had drawn an absurd picture of a sheet with eyeholes. The other had drawn a blob of dough with a tuft of hair. What did they know about ghosts? Nothing. Neither drawing looked like it had ever been human, once upon a time.

The pencil slipped from Hannah's fingers and rolled across the floor, scaring a mouse. The notebook fell from Anna's hand. A blank page blew to cover up their drawings. There. That was better.

Hannah opened her eyes. She stared across the room. Sometimes it was easier to see things in the dark. Other people had found that to be true in the house. That was why they left. No one cared about them. Even if they had brought fascinating books, no one would have ever hoped they would stay. No one would have wanted them as friends.

Slowly Hannah lifted her head and propped herself up on her left elbow. She blinked. Beyond the lump of Anna under the blankets, Hannah could see shadowy shapes. The flap on the box wasn't waggling anymore. She held her breath to listen. All she heard was Anna's breathing—and the pounding of her own heart.

She shouldn't be afraid. No one wanted to hurt her. She should go back to sleep. When the sun shone, the house wouldn't seem so gloomy. In the morning, she would accept the fact that she had to stay.

Finally Hannah put her head back on the pillow and curved her body around Anna. The two girls fit together as precisely as the pieces of a jigsaw puzzle.

And yet there was room for something to slip between them.

The next day, a man with tools knocked on the door and asked for Mr. Zimmer. So that was the family's name.

"I'm glad you could come so quickly," Mr. Zimmer said.

"I bet you are. In a place like this, you need a phone to call for help," the man with tools said.

He strung a new wire from the telephone pole into the house. He ran another wire into the kitchen, where the telephone had always been. This new telephone didn't hang on the wall. It sat on the kitchen counter. Its numbers were on buttons. And it had a shiny silver antenna.

The first telephone call was for Selena. "Hello," she squealed. She didn't stay in the kitchen, where her mother could hear what she was saying and her younger sisters could supply sound effects. Selena took the phone up to her room and shut the door. She flopped onto her bed and gushed to her friend about the big house in the cute town and how huge her bedroom was.

She neglected to mention the shut door at the far end of the bedroom. Or what was behind it. In fact, she had forgotten all about it. Her thoughts were a boring jumble of who liked who and who didn't like who and who would like who if only someone knew who didn't like who. It didn't matter what she thought or what she did— until she put down the phone and took an armful of coats over to the closet.

Would she go in there again?

A small breeze lifted the hairs along her bare arms. She dropped the coats.

"I'm all right," she said. As if anyone in the room cared.

She thought how she didn't need a closet. She hadn't had one in Brooklyn. She would have a beautiful new closet in the new house. Until then, she could make do. She put the coats back in the WARDROBE box and spent the rest of the morning covering the drab brown sides with pictures of handsome men.

Downstairs, Mr. Zimmer was trying to find places to plug in everything. Since he couldn't, his thoughts weren't very nice. Almost everything they owned had cords— including Mrs. Zimmer's sewing machine. She put it in the dining room next to the big table. Where would the family eat if that was her work space? She wasn't thinking about meals. She rolled a dressmaker's dummy in front of the dining room window. It had the curves of a woman but no head—just like a silly teenage girl. Ha!

Where were Hannah and Anna? They weren't reading *The Golden Compass* and *The Subtle Knife* anymore. That was good. Those books were too unsettling for those who really had been cut off from loved ones.

Why didn't Hannah and Anna get a book like *The Story of the Treasure Seekers*? Yes, the Bastable children had their sorrows. Their mother was dead and their father had lost his money. The children were always getting into trouble. Like the time they made the neighbor boy Albert dig for treasure and he nearly got buried alive. The Bastables squabbled too, because Dora was so bossy and acted like she was better than the others. But in the end, everything came right. What was the point of reading a book if it didn't?

Maybe the book that followed *The Subtle Knife* had a happy ending. Maybe it was in the box upstairs. If only the twins would stop whispering in their room and unpack the rest of their books.

Anna picked up a sheet that should have been on her bed and put it over Hannah's head. It wasn't even white. She looked like a walking rainbow.

"Whooo. Whooo," Hannah said.

"You sound like an owl."

"What should I say?"

"Something to scare her."

Hannah spoke in a deep, hollow voice. "Seleeeenaaaa, yoooou look fat in those jeeeeeeans."

The twins laughed—until their mother opened the door.

"Knock first!" the twins yelled.

Mrs. Zimmer knocked twice on the open door, came straight in, and yanked the sheet off Hannah. "Didn't I tell you not to tease Selena?"

"We're only playing," Anna said.

"Well, stop. You haven't unpacked one single thing," Mrs. Zimmer said.

The twins fidgeted with the sheet. Even their mother knew they were up to something. She just didn't know what.

"Why won't you? You'll feel better if you get out your books," Mrs. Zimmer said.

Yes, everybody would.

"School starts in less than a week," Mrs. Zimmer said.

Of course, all children had to go to school—if they could go. School wasn't so bad for girls like Hannah and Anna. But Hannah was worried. "Why can't we be in the same class like we were in Brooklyn?" she said.

"The principal believes that twins gain more independence when they're encouraged to reach out to others," Mrs. Zimmer said.

The twins thought those words were babble.

Mrs. Zimmer tried again. "Just think of all the new friends you'll make."

"We have friends," Anna said.

"In Brooklyn," Hannah said.

"You can make more friends," Mrs. Zimmer said.

It was true. They could—if they would only stop paying so much attention to each other.

"Should I buy us a treat at the cute little bakery on Main Street? Your dad is going out to buy more extension cords," Mrs. Zimmer said.

"Something chocolate?" Anna said.

"Of course," Mrs. Zimmer said.

Then Hannah thought of something. If the parents were gone, she and Anna had an opportunity to scare Selena. "Is Selena going?"

"To a hardware store?" Mrs. Zimmer said.

They all laughed. Mrs. Zimmer hugged her daughters and left.

Hannah pulled the sheet over their heads and whispered to Anna.

After a few moments, two car doors slammed. An engine roared to life. Gravel crunched under the tires.

The house was quiet. A few greedy mice scampered out into the kitchen, even though not everyone had left.

Selena was trying on an outfit she planned to wear on the first day of school. She looked very strange. Other children never had new clothes. Not once. At least those hand-me-down dresses weren't torn. The shorts Selena put on were frayed at the bottom and faded on the thighs. Her shirt had so many holes, she had to wear it over another shirt. Even then, the straps of her brassiere showed. She didn't have shoes on her feet, just rubber soles with straps between the toes. And yet she primped and pranced in front of the mirror on her dresser, delighted with how she looked.

"Hannah Anna, I've decided what I'm going to wear. Now I can help you."

She knocked on their door. The twins didn't answer.

"You need to plan ahead. First impressions are very important. Since it's a brand-new school, this is your *first* first impression. You can be somebody totally new and cool. Wouldn't that be great? Hannah Anna?"

Selena opened their door. Nobody was there.

"Did you go to the hardware store? You really are nerds." She shrugged and sashayed back along the hall.

Where were the twins? There was a squeak on the attic steps. Selena didn't notice. She was thinking that she was alone in the house so she could do whatever she wanted to do. She was thinking there were cookies in the kitchen. Then she scolded herself to resist temptation and hurried back into her room.

Meanwhile, careful feet crept up the attic steps.

Hannah and Anna pulled themselves up along the railing until they reached the top. Their hearts pounded with nervous excitement. They could hardly see anything. Their eyes hadn't adjusted to the dark. The only light came in through the cracks under the eaves.

Once upon a time, the attic had been full of treasures. In the corner above the parents' bedroom, a pile of old rugs could be a magic carpet or Huck Finn's raft or something to hide behind. A barrel of mismatched dishes were perfect for tea parties. A trunk could be a table. Next to the chimney were boxes of old photos, Christmas ornaments, wooden skis, a lamp that didn't work, a wooden high chair, and a homemade rocking horse.

The attic had no treasures now. Everything in it had been carted away. Except one thing. One precious thing had been hidden below the floor next to the eaves when all the books in the smallest bedroom were being taken away. Not a living soul knew where it was—not even the critters. For almost eighty years, no one had been able to take it out and look at it. But now that girls were here, maybe . . .

"Now what?" Anna whispered.

"I find the spot above Selena's closet." Hannah walked toward the center of the attic. She waved her hands in front of her to feel her way through the darkness. The space was nearly the size of the whole house. There were no walls.

"You think here?" Hannah whispered.

"Farther," Anna whispered.

Hannah stopped. She sensed something stirring in the darkness above her head. She knew she and Anna weren't the only ones in the attic. She just didn't know who else was there.

"What is it?" Anna whispered.

Hannah wasn't sure. She was listening. Was there enough silence? Maybe she would go and find the precious thing.

Look.

Anna was too impatient. "Hurry up," she whispered.

So Hannah stopped listening and sat on the floor. It was very dirty. She lifted her feet and kicked the boards with the heels of her shoes.

BOMP, BOMP, BOMP. Slow, deliberate thumps, like the drums in the parades that honored the soldiers on Armistice Day.

The sound woke up all the bats. They unfurled their wings and dropped from the rafters. They swooped around the attic.

The twins didn't appreciate the dance. Hannah rolled onto her stomach. Anna crouched on the floor. They both covered their heads with their arms.

Too bad they couldn't enjoy Selena's screams as she ran from the sound, down the stairs, and into the kitchen. Ha!

Back in the attic, the bats swirled. The twins didn't dare move as long as they felt the whoosh of wings. Finally the bats realized it was too early to hunt. They returned to their naps.

When Mr. and Mrs. Zimmer came home, they found Selena lying on the sofa, holding her stomach and moaning.

"What's wrong?" Mrs. Zimmer dropped the bag of baked goods and rushed to her daughter's side.

"I heard a noise coming from my closet," Selena said.

"There's going to be noises in an old house," Mr. Zimmer said.

"I'm sure it was nothing," Mrs. Zimmer said.

"Then something really terrible happened!" Selena wailed.

The twins clattered down the stairs and into the living room.

"What's wrong?" Anna said.

"What happened?" Hannah said.

The twins were thinking how well their plan had worked—until Selena finally managed to say, "I ate all the chocolate-chip cookies."

"Is that all?" Mr. Zimmer said.

"I can't wear these shorts on the first day. I know I gained at least ten pounds." Selena said.

"You couldn't have. A package of cookies only weighs one pound," Mr. Zimmer said.

Mrs. Zimmer was staring at the twins. "What's on your clothes?"

Hannah and Anna looked down at the dark powder on their shirts.

"How did you get so filthy?" Mrs. Zimmer said.

"We were outside," Anna said.

"Playing," Hannah said.

"That is not outside dirt. Where have you been?" Mrs. Zimmer said.

"You were up in the attic," Selena said.

Apparently she wasn't as dumb as people thought.

"You made the thumping noise. You scared me into eating all those cookies. I hate you! I hate you both!"

"How could you do that to your sister?" Mrs. Zimmer was thinking the twins were driving her crazy.

"How could you make us move to this house?" Hannah said.

"You know perfectly well why." Mr. Zimmer was thinking he was sick of their complaints.

"You don't care about us," Anna said.

"You only care about her," Hannah said.

"That isn't true," Selena said.

Yes, it was. And everybody in the house knew it.

❊ 6 ❊

Mr. and Mrs. Zimmer didn't make the twins cut a switch for playing that trick on Selena. Nobody took away their books. However, Hannah and Anna were punished. For the next two days, Selena followed them everywhere, asking if she had lost any weight yet or if her thighs still looked too big to wear shorts. Finally the twins went outside to escape. They walked purposefully down the driveway. They stopped next to the oldest tree at the edge of Hemlock Road.

What was the matter? Couldn't they leave the property? Was this their punishment too?

They looked toward the right. The trees blocked the view of the old lady's house. They looked left. The road curved before they could see the stone gates that guarded the driveway that snaked up the hill to the fancy house, where no one was allowed to go.

"Where's the sidewalk?" Hannah said.

"I hate that we have to be driven everywhere," Anna said.

"Especially since Dad can't," Hannah said.

Mr. Zimmer had taken a train to his job.

"And Mom won't," Anna said.

Mrs. Zimmer was cutting cloth on what should have been a dining room table.

"I guess I'll have to learn to drive," Anna said.

"In five years," Hannah said.

The twins sighed. They were thinking of that other street—the one lined with cute shops instead of gloomy trees.

One branch swayed, as if to say, *We understand how you feel. Please don't blame us. We can't help the way we are.*

Hannah watched it. She wondered why it moved when all the rest were still. "Remember the first day, when the tree waved? Why does it do that?"

She was asking Anna, even though Anna didn't know or care. She had spotted one of the cats slinking past the porch under the red chokeberry bush.

"Ooh, a kitty," Anna said. Both twins ran after it.

The gray one, with the white front paws, wasn't the meanest or the ugliest. But like all cats, it searched for a defenseless critter to kill.

"Is it a stray?" Hannah said.

"It doesn't have a collar," Anna said.

"Maybe we can keep it," they said together, and excitedly clasped hands.

Didn't they know what a cat could do?

"Here, kitty," Anna said.

"Here, Muffie," Hannah said.

"Is that its name?" Anna thought that sounded a little childish.

"How about Mr. Muffin?" Hannah said.

The cat, who should be named Mr. Murderer, raced around the side of the house. The twins followed.

"Wait, Mr. Muffin," Anna said.

The backyard was even more neglected than the front. Once upon a time, there had been a garden. A mother had planted seeds and the seeds had become vegetables that she made her children eat. One October, long ago, squash rotted on the vines. No one was there to pick the Halloween pumpkin and carve a face that could scare away the devil.

The cat had spotted a brown bird pecking at the dirt under a bush. The bird cocked its head to one side and hopped. The cat crouched very low to the ground, inching forward, one white paw at a time. The bird didn't see the danger. The twins should be paying attention. They should do something. It was very wrong to let an innocent critter die. One little death could lead to another.

The gray tail lashed back and forth. Just as the cat coiled itself to pounce, a gust of wind rustled the leaves right above the bird. It flapped away. It had been saved.

Hannah and Anna didn't notice that—or how close they were getting to the place.

Some places were powerful because of what had

happened there. Some were powerful because of what hadn't. The twins walked toward a place that was both.

Did they realize that? No. Anna was planning how to persuade their parents to get a cat. Even Hannah was thinking that it was pleasant to be outside instead of in the gloomy old house.

How could they know? The place looked like a field, bordered on the south edge by large gray rocks. The grass was beautiful. The golden stalks swayed in a gentle breeze. And yet something had happened in the shadow of those rocks. It changed the place forever. It could never be forgiven. It was the worst thing that could be done to anyone. Then other people covered everything up with dirt. Yes, dirt. They didn't want anyone to see the place and remember. So no one ever did.

The twins paused. They had reached the edge of the deep ditch. Would they cross it? Could they? Or would they be stuck pacing back and forth and back and forth?

"That's weird." Hannah shivered as she looked down. "There's a path down there."

Anna was still thinking about the cat. "So?"

"Why would somebody walk along the bottom of the ditch?"

Why was she wondering about that? There were other, more important questions that needed answers. Like where was justice, and where was the way out of the . . .

"There goes Mr. Muffin," Anna said.

The cat ran down into the ditch and up the other side.

Anna ran after it. Just like that, she left the yard, without even trying, without even noticing.

Hannah followed her sister. Maybe there was a way to go with her and cross the line. She was a girl who sometimes seemed to understand.

But no.

Nothing had changed.

Hannah ran up the other side of the ditch. From there, she had a closer view of the yellow field and the strange sapling that grew just beyond the rocks. She thought the red lines in its leaves looked like blood flowing through veins.

One of its branches moved.

"It's waving," Hannah said.

No, it wasn't. It wasn't sending a signal. It truly was the wind. Couldn't Hannah tell the difference?

"It wants me to come closer."

No, it didn't.

Hannah walked until she stood just a few feet from the edge.

"Are you talking about the cat?" Anna said.

"The tree," Hannah said.

Anna thought that was ridiculous. Then she spotted the cat creeping into the golden grass. "There goes Mr. Muffin."

"Where?" Hannah said.

The cat disappeared except for the tip of its gray tail. Its tail stopped moving. For a moment, everything was still. Even the wind held its breath, waiting to see what would happen.

Suddenly the cat yowled and sprang back from the field. It darted past the twins. Its tail was puffed. Its ears were flat. And its sleek gray body was covered with black muck.

The cat darted past the twins' legs, away from the field. Both girls followed it down the ditch, up the other side, and past the dead garden. The cat scrambled halfway up an ash tree and clung to the trunk. It was safe now. But its eyes were wild and it was still afraid.

The twins stopped under it. Anna held up her hands. She wanted to bring it down, but she couldn't reach it.

"What's that smell?" Hannah said.

The muck on the cat's legs smelled like rotting decay. Like death. Because that was what it was.

"Poor Mr. Muffin. Would you let us give you a bath?" Anna said.

The family car pulled into the driveway. Mrs. Zimmer had picked Mr. Zimmer up at the train station.

The twins ran over to their parents. "We found a cat, can we keep it?"

Mrs. Zimmer thought a cat might be a good idea. Those mice had nibbled too many boxes. The twins led their parents to where the cat still clung to the tree.

"It's filthy," Mrs. Zimmer said.

"I thought cats were clean," Mr. Zimmer said.

"Mr. Muffin *was* clean," Anna said.

"Until he went in a mucky place in our backyard," Hannah said.

"There isn't a mucky place in our backyard." Like so many people, Mr. Zimmer never considered what might lurk below the surface.

"The ground is very dry." Mrs. Zimmer pointed to what used to be the garden. "I couldn't even dig."

"Were you going to plant something?" Mr. Zimmer said.

"I just hate looking at the weeds," Mrs. Zimmer said.

"There is a mucky, stinky, dangerous place behind the house that no one should live near," Hannah said. She was thinking she had a new reason to get her parents to move. Would they listen to her? Would they take their daughters away?

"Where?" Mr. Zimmer said.

Hannah dragged him to the edge of the ditch and pointed at the field. "There."

"That's not our yard," Mr. Zimmer said. "The property line is the ditch. You shouldn't go anywhere near that field."

That was what people always said. You shouldn't have been there. If you had listened to me, this would never have happened. That's what you get for not obeying the rules. Everybody blamed the victim for being in the wrong place at the wrong time.

Hannah was wondering what was hidden by the grass—until Anna said, "Can we keep the cat?"

"Can we?" Hannah said.

"We'll see," Mr. Zimmer said.

"If it cleans itself up." Mrs. Zimmer said.

The parents went into the house.

"I don't think Mr. Muffin should lick that," Hannah said.

"Why not?" Anna said. "Cats lick dirt all the time."

"Not that dirt," Hannah said.

"Isn't dirt dirt?" Anna said.

Hannah knew this dirt was different, although she didn't know why.

After dinner, the twins went upstairs. Tomorrow was the first day of school. Both twins were so excited, their thoughts bounced around too much to read as they filled their new backpacks. Anna's was lime green with blue stitching. Hannah's was orange with red stitching. All the pens and notebooks were brightly colored too. School must be much more fun now—if one was allowed to go.

"I'll sharpen the pencils." Anna grabbed both boxes.

"I'll help you," Hannah said.

"There's only one sharpener. I'll be right back." Anna ran downstairs.

Hannah stood in the doorway. Why was she nervous

about staying in the room? She thought that was silly. It was even sillier to feel nervous about school. School was school—even if sometimes the teachers arranged the desks in a circle. She always liked school, especially if there were decent books. But she couldn't help thinking that when she walked into the classroom tomorrow, she wouldn't have Anna.

She turned away from the door. The dark outside made a mirror out of the window. There was her face behind the glass. Now she could see how anxious she felt.

Beyond that face was the field. She couldn't see it. She didn't need to—she remembered the ditch where someone used to walk and the tree with red leaves and the golden grass growing on top of stinky muck.

She wondered why the field was so mucky. She wondered if it was a wetland. She reminded herself that wetlands were good. Wetlands were supposed to be saved and protected. She had learned that at school. So why had the cat been so frightened?

It must have seen a snake or a fox or an alligator escaped from a zoo. Hannah would have believed a sensible explanation, if she hadn't been standing in a room in the house on Hemlock Road.

Hannah couldn't sleep until she got out one of her old favorite books to read. *Charlotte's Web* was really "terrific"—ha! The critters in the house would have been very impressed that someone had written a book whose heroine was a spider.

When morning came, Hannah put the book in her backpack. It would hardly make up for not having Anna.

"No one will even know we're twins," Hannah said.

"Duh." Anna pointed to their faces. She was wondering why Hannah was so anxious. She never used to be.

"They won't know if they don't see us together and we won't *be* together. We should show them we aren't ashamed of being twins," Hannah said.

"How?"

"We'll dress alike."

Hannah was so insistent that Anna agreed, even though she remembered what Selena had said about first first impressions.

After Selena left for her school, the twins came downstairs in identical crimson dresses with white lace collars. Another girl wore a dress like that, once upon a time. Except the twins' wrists stuck out two inches from the ends of their sleeves and their skirts came nowhere near their knees. Whenever they breathed, small rips sprouted around their waists.

"Why on earth are you wearing the dresses your grandma bought you three Christmases ago?" Mrs. Zimmer said.

"Twins dress alike," Hannah said.

"You never wanted to before," Mrs. Zimmer said.

"You never split us up before," Hannah said.

"You should have told me. I could have made you something cute," Mrs. Zimmer said.

"We did tell you," Anna said.

"We wanted to be together," Hannah said.

"You never listen to us."

"Just to Selena."

Mrs. Zimmer sighed. "I'll make you identical tops you can wear tomorrow. Run upstairs and find some clothes that fit."

Anna thought that would solve the problem. She hurried back up the stairs. Unfortunately there wasn't time to change. One of the big yellow buses that always zipped past the house on Hemlock Road screeched to a halt at the end of the driveway and opened its door. Someone in the back of the bus shouted, "Why did we stop at the house with green eyes?"

It was a boy. Boys were the ones who usually bothered the house, especially at Halloween. A long time ago, the green eyes appeared when those boys threw rocks. The shattered glass hurt so much. Like another insult. Another injury. Didn't those boys realize that things were bad enough? They didn't know or care. Then years passed. Broken windows became a nuisance. The green eyes faded into a joke. Had this boy with round cheeks been to the house? Had he made a mad dash to touch the glass where the eyes used to appear? Perhaps.

The branch of the hemlock waved. The boy kept right on talking. "What kind of kids would live here? Nobody would—except insane people."

The driver honked the horn.

The house's front door opened. Hannah and Anna came out and walked side by side toward the bus. Hannah was nervous, but she knew better than to hold Anna's hand.

The round-cheeked boy howled when he saw them. "Those *are* loonies from the loony bin. I bet they dress alike because they belong to a cult. They're disciples of the green eyes."

As Hannah and Anna climbed the steps to the bus, they were met by the roar of children laughing. This had never happened to them before. They were so shocked; they stood frozen by the driver.

"Sit down, disciples!" the round-cheeked boy yelled. "Don't make us late for school."

"You sit down, Hubert. You talk too much," said a girl with too many red curls. "Hey, new girls. Come sit by me."

Hannah slid into a seat across from the redheaded girl. Anna sat right next to the girl. Anna thought this was only right because the girl had stood up for them. Anna smiled at the redheaded girl. Didn't she care that Hannah was sitting by herself?

Maybe Hannah wouldn't have to stay alone.

The bus was parked right at the edge of the driveway. The window next to Hannah was open. It looked like a crack into a new world. It looked like anyone could slip through the gap, into the bus and away.

It hadn't been possible to leave yesterday. It had been too near the potent place. Today was different. There couldn't be anything wrong with going to school with the girls. Maybe after all these years . . .

But the bus drove away. No one could follow it. No one.

It hurt a little more this time, because there had been hoping. And now Hannah would have to be alone.

The branch of the hemlock tree waved good-bye, good luck. Hannah was going to need it.

Inside the house, Mrs. Zimmer sketched a shirt with a diagonal neck. She muttered as she erased the lines and drew again.

"They should have told me they wanted to dress alike. A designer's daughters can't go to school in rags."

She chose a piece of bright turquoise cloth from the shelves built into the walls of the dining room. Once upon a time those shelves had been crowded with good china used only on Christmas and birthdays. Bit by bit, the china had disappeared. Had it been sold when the father couldn't find work? The parents never said. The cake plate was the only thing left. Then one day, the father banged the dining room table with both hands and shouted for silence. The plate wobbled off the shelf and smashed on the floor. The mother never made cake again. Not even for birthdays.

Mrs. Zimmer shook out the cloth. It billowed up and then fell across the table.

"This will be nice," she said.

The phone rang.

"Hi, Samantha," Mrs. Zimmer said.

Samantha, whoever she was, urgently needed something to wear to an opening, whatever that was.

"I know just the thing." Mrs. Zimmer hung up the phone and made a new drawing. Just like that, her daughters' tops became a stranger's dress.

Hannah and Anna were the ones who needed to be admired. Who cared about that other woman?

Mrs. Zimmer cut the cloth. Snip, snip, snip. She held the scissors in her right hand. She steadied the cloth with her left. A strange wind made the cloth billow up.

"Hey!" She struggled to uncover her face.

It was too late. The cut had been made. The fabric was ruined.

When she saw what she had done, she said something very rude and crude.

That was no way for a mother to talk. Who knew Mrs. Zimmer had such a temper?

She wadded up the cloth and threw it at the dress-maker's dummy. Ha!

Outside, in the only sunny spot in the front yard, Mr. Murderer was licking himself with his rough pink tongue. His gray fur was still tinged with brown. If he hadn't been a cat, some might have felt sorry for him. Every few moments, he gagged and tried to cough something up.

It wasn't pleasant to watch. There was nothing else to do while waiting for the yellow bus to bring back the twins. Even though it was just a few hours, time passed much more slowly than it had for years.

Finally the bus stopped at the end of the driveway. Hannah ran down the steps. Anna followed more slowly. She turned back to say, "See you tomorrow, Georgia," to the redheaded girl.

Hannah flopped down on the front yard. School had made her so unhappy, she was glad to be back at the house on Hemlock Road. "The longest day of our lives."

It had seemed that way for others too—but not for Anna. In fact, Anna looked cool and refreshed. The sleeves had been cut off her dress. Her arms were bare.

"Why did you let Georgia do that to your dress?" Hannah said.

"Isn't it a fun idea?" Anna thought she was lucky to have Georgia in her class. "I got so hot at recess."

"Playing kickball," Hannah said bitterly.

"Why didn't you play?"

"I was waiting for you by the fence."

"I was waiting for you to come and play."

Hannah plucked at the lawn that was more dirt than grass.

"Did you make any friends?" Anna said.

Hannah shook her head. She thought how everyone in her class seemed to have friends already.

"How's your teacher?" Anna said.

"Ms. Debaremdiker doesn't think we can pronounce her name. She wants us to call her Miz D. She talks in a loud, cheerful voice like a kindergarten teacher. She got mad at me because when she made us write our goals, I wrote, *Not to go back*."

Anna laughed, until she saw that Hannah meant it. "You have to go to school."

"I'd rather die."

Of course people always said that. Until they were dead.

The hemlock branch waved, *shush, shush, shush*. That didn't change Hannah's mind. More than anything, she wanted to go back to Brooklyn.

"That's not all. She called me up in front of the whole

class to say I had a bad attitude. And having a bad attitude was a self-fulfilling prophecy," Hannah said.

"You mean if you think bad things, bad things will happen to you?" Anna said.

"Yes," Hannah said.

"That might be true," Anna said.

It was wrong to blame the victim. How could Anna say that? Everyone else could see how unhappy Hannah was.

Hannah couldn't forget how she felt at school without Anna, surrounded by children but utterly alone. Like nobody could see her or hear her. Like she watched them from behind a window.

So now she knew what that was like.

Another school bus stopped at the end of the driveway.

"Maybe Selena had a wonderfully horrible bad day too." This cheered Hannah up. If she had been mocked, she could imagine what must have happened to her silly sister.

Selena floated dreamily down the steps and drifted toward the house without even seeing the twins.

"How was your day?" Anna called.

"The high school kids are probably really mean, aren't they?" Hannah said.

Selena came over to the twins. "What are you wearing? Are those the dresses Grandma bought you three Christmases ago?"

Anna sighed. She knew she shouldn't have let Hannah talk her into wearing it.

"What happened to the outfits I helped you pick out?" Selena said.

"So we changed. So what? We want to hear about your day. Your teachers probably gave you stacks of homework," Hannah said.

"I get to read *The Diary of Anne Frank* again," Selena said.

"You won't learn anything," Anna said.

"You'll be *bored*," Hannah said.

Both twins thought that was the worst thing possible.

"No, I won't. Since I already know it, I'll be smart," Selena said.

"You won't ever be smart," Hannah said.

"At least I'm smart enough not to wear an ugly dress to school," Selena said.

Now the sisters would quarrel and Hannah's misery would spread to Selena.

But Anna said, "What else happened?"

Selena sat down with her sisters and flipped her long golden hair back over her left shoulder and then her right. "I was on my way to my last class. I had to hurry because I didn't want to be late again."

"Wasn't that embarrassing?" Anna said.

Selena smiled. "It's one way to get noticed."

"For having a big butt," Hannah said.

Selena ignored that remark. "Someone was hurrying more than me. When I stopped to check the room number, I got knocked down."

"Don't you hate being stuck in a boring school with bullies?" Hannah said.

"This bully has dark eyes and a gap between his bottom teeth that you can only see when he smiles." Selena sighed and flung open her arms like she wanted to hug the whole world. "I can't wait for history tomorrow."

The pretty ones always got all the joy. Poor Hannah in her hot dress fell back on the grass and groaned.

The week went by. Every night at dinner, Mr. Zimmer said, "Today was better, right?" And every night Selena and Anna would say yes, because it was better for them. Marcus sat next to Selena in history class. Georgia gave Anna a book she said Anna *had* to read. Marcus smiled at Selena in the cafeteria. Georgia and Anna got to take the attendance card to the office. Better and better for everyone in the whole world—except Hannah and those who truly cared about her.

Why didn't she go back to the attic? Others also found the bats scary at first, but being lonely was much worse than being afraid. Besides, the bats only ate insects. They couldn't harm anything else. They were misunderstood too.

Night after night, Hannah just lay on her bunk. Her ceiling was the attic floor. She was so close to that precious hidden thing. So close to the dance. She never even looked at the dark window now. Tonight she played with a dried noodle she wore around her neck.

"Hannah?" Anna said. "Are you mad?"

"No." Hannah wasn't mad at Anna. Not even just a little. Hannah blamed that girl Georgia. She thought Georgia was making Anna care about strange things like being popular.

"Why *were* you wearing that piece of pasta?" Anna said.

Pasta was what the Zimmers had called those pink and green noodles shaped like wagon wheels. Mrs. Zimmer had unpacked them from one of the boxes they brought from Brooklyn. When Hannah saw the noodles, she had nearly cried as she said, "From the Food Co-op?" Whatever that was.

"How could you even ask me? It's the last piece from Brooklyn. Mom cooked the rest. So there isn't any more and there won't be until we move back."

Anna sighed. She thought Hannah wasn't even trying to get along here.

"It did look cool. You thought so—until Georgia said, 'What's your sister wearing around her neck? We made pasta jewelry in kindergarten.'" Hannah tried to make her voice sound like Georgia's.

"She was teasing you. We made pasta jewelry in kindergarten too," Anna said.

Hannah didn't say anything more. She knew Georgia looked for ways to make fun of her to drive her away. Then Georgia could have Anna all to herself at recess.

Hannah didn't want to be with them either. Anna had dragged her over to the kickball game. Hannah knew Anna was trying to help. But being there made Hannah feel worse. It showed how Anna had made friends and she hadn't.

Hannah was wrong. She did have friends. She just couldn't see them or hear them. Maybe one day she would.

Finally Saturday arrived. There was no school. The twins would be home all day. After their chores were done, they could read books and draw pictures. If they climbed the second hemlock, they could spy in their sister's bedroom window.

They didn't do any of those things because Mr. Zimmer said, "Who needs to go to the mall?"

"We do," Anna said.

"We do?" Hannah said.

"We need more books, and batteries for our flashlights," Anna said.

Anna didn't say what else she was thinking. She also wanted to buy cute tops so that Hannah would stop wearing the shirt with the words PARK SLOPE. Anna was also thinking they might run into Georgia.

Didn't Anna know that Hannah wouldn't like that? Obviously Anna didn't care about her twin. So Hannah shouldn't go with her. Hannah should stay.

Stay.

Hannah put on her shoes and walked down the stairs. She saw something reflected in the hall tree mirror. That glimpse didn't make her change her mind. It just made her fuss with her hair.

Then they were going. They were leaving. Mr. and Mrs. Zimmer were already in the car.

Wait.

Hannah didn't wait. She didn't understand. She was shutting the front door.

"Make sure it's locked," Mrs. Zimmer called.

Did they want to keep something out? Or something in?

The phone rang. Selena practically knocked her sisters over as she ran back into the house. The call was for her.

Marcus asked her to go to the movies with him that night.

She said yes and hung up the phone.

There hadn't been so much screaming in the house on Hemlock Road since the first day—when Selena went in the closet.

All that screaming gave Hannah an idea. It wasn't a good idea. It was a dangerous idea. However, it did make Hannah change her mind.

She stood at the foot of the stairs looking up toward Selena's room.

"Hurry up, Hannah," Selena said.

"I'm not going," Hannah said.

"Why not?" Anna came back inside. "You have to go. You said you were."

Hannah shook her head. "I just realized. There's something I need to do."

❧ 10 ❧

"What?" Anna said. "What are you going to do?"

Hannah didn't say. She was thinking that she couldn't, not with Selena standing right there. She didn't have to tell Anna everything anymore. And maybe she didn't want to.

Anna wondered why Hannah was acting like this. "Why won't you tell me?"

"Let Hannah stay if she wants to. We have to go. Marcus is picking me up at seven. That's in . . ."

Selena's brain got tangled with numbers until Anna said, "Four hours and twenty-three minutes." Selena hugged her sister happily and ran back to the car.

"Go," Hannah said.

"No," Anna said.

The twins stared at each other stubbornly. The horn honked. Anna went outside and called to her parents, "I'm staying home with Hannah!"

After the sounds of the car had faded, Hannah went upstairs into Selena's room. Anna followed her. Clothes were everywhere. It looked like whatever was in the closet had burst out and wrecked the room. This disaster was caused by a vain teenage girl who couldn't decide what to wear.

"Why come in here? Are you going to read her diary?" Anna was thinking that Selena probably hadn't written in it since she and Hannah read it five years ago.

"No. I'm going to use what's in her closet to scare her," Hannah said.

Use it? Did she really think she could control what she would feel in the closet?

"She has a boyfriend now. She won't want to move back to Brooklyn no matter what you do," Anna said.

Hannah pushed aside piles of clothes with her foot to clear a path to the closet. Mr. Zimmer had hung a mirror on the door. Now Selena only thought about how she looked. She never considered what was behind the glass.

"You should stop trying to scare Selena," Anna said.

Anna was right. Hannah should stop. The closet was no place for pranks.

Hannah didn't agree. "You liked the idea last week."

"That was before."

"Before you changed."

Anna looked down at her shirt, even though she knew perfectly well that Hannah meant something else. "You're right. Going to the mall was a dumb idea. But so is scaring Selena. Let's find something fun to do. I know. We can look for Mr. Muffin."

Hannah shook her head. She grabbed the knob and turned it. Slowly she opened the closet door. She paused just outside, squinting at the darkness, as if she were looking at a very bright light.

She wasn't, of course. She was looking at a bad place. It wasn't as dreadful as what lay behind the house, but it was where the terrible events began.

What would happen if she went inside? Would she understand? And even if she did, then what? Would that change everything? Or just her?

Hannah took a deep breath and stepped into the closet.

After she disappeared into the darkness, Anna followed her.

They stood in the center, listening to their breathing. Anna held her nose to keep out the smell. "How long do we have to stay here?" Anna whispered.

"Be quiet."

Hannah was trying to listen. She really was. There was so much to say. It was hard to describe how everything went wrong. Not without getting angry all over again.

It was wrong to punish one deed and not the other. Letting a little critter die is a crime much worse than ruining a few fancy dresses. Much, much worse. Didn't people realize that anyone who watches one thing die would gladly watch another?

"Nothing's happening," Anna said.

"That's because you're talking, so shut up."

Then Hannah did something she shouldn't have. She shut the door. Now they were utterly in the dark.

"What did you do that for?" Anna said.

"I need to concentrate."

The girls found it hard to breathe. There was a limited supply of air—and love. Some people say it's infinite. But there isn't nearly enough to make up for the hate. The twins were discovering that—even though they didn't realize it.

"I'm leaving," Anna said.

"What are you going to do? Call Georgia?"

Actually Anna was going to call Georgia.

"Are you going to complain that I kept you from going to the mall?"

"You *did* keep me from going."

"So?"

"So don't ask to borrow my flashlight when your batteries run out."

"I won't borrow anything of yours ever again."

"Yes, you will. You always need my help."

"No, I don't. I don't want you here. You're in the way."

Anna stumbled toward the door. It was too dark to see the way out. "I can't find the knob." Anna's voice cracked.

Hannah came and found it. For some reason it was stuck.

"It won't turn." Hannah pushed the door with both hands. Then she quickly stepped back.

Ah. Her fingers had found the deep gouge in the wood.

"There's something carved in the door," Hannah whispered.

Anna felt her way along Hannah's arm and put her hand next to Hannah's. Together they traced the rough edges. The line was about six inches long.

"What is it?" Anna said.

It marked what had been done—and who had done it.

Hannah cautiously explored the wood until her hand touched another scratch just as deep and long, only this one bent. "It's writing. It's an *I* and an *L*."

"Maybe it spells *I Love You?*" Anna said.

Who would write that to a murderer?

They looked for the *O V E,* but these were the letters they found:

ILDRED

"Ildred," Hannah said.

Ha! Why not call the monster that? It was a fitting name. Much better than the real one.

"We should never have come in here. Why did you make me?" Anna said.

"You followed me," Hannah said.

"I was trying to keep you out of trouble," Anna said.

"You're the one who broke the door," Hannah said.

"You're the one who slammed it shut," Anna said.

"Stop blaming me," Hannah said.

"You started it," Anna said.

"So now you really hate me, don't you?" Hannah said.

She shouldn't have said that. One hate always bred another in the house on Hemlock Road—like more and more and more mice.

"Don't you?" Hannah said again.

"It's your fault we're stuck in here with Ildred," Anna said.

"Don't say its name. What if it comes?"

That green-eyed monster had already done its damage—ILDRED was there.

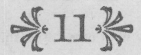

11

Hannah and Anna inched as far from the door as possible. When they got to the closet's back wall, they sank down to the floor and sat in opposite corners. They weren't speaking to each other. Spiteful thoughts screamed inside their heads.

They were trapped. Would that help them understand how others felt, stuck next to the worst possible place? No—even Hannah was just feeling sorry for herself.

Why should *they* complain? Their family hadn't driven away and left them forever. Their family was going to return. Their darkness only seemed eternal. Eventually someone would open the closet door and let them out.

"Why aren't they back?" Anna said.

"How should I know?" Hannah said.

Anna said nothing.

"You can't blame that on me too," Hannah said.

"I wasn't," Anna said.

"Yes, you were. I know what you're thinking," Hannah said.

Did she know what others were thinking? Could she know?

Hannah wriggled. She couldn't get comfortable. This wasn't surprising. She was stuck in a hot, stinky, dark place just inches from someone who didn't like her very much at the moment.

Anna sat with her eyes shut, humming a song that reminded her of Georgia.

"Ow." Hannah had put her palm down on something small and sharp. It stuck to her damp skin. She picked it up with her other hand and held it between her thumb and forefinger.

What was it?

"I found something," Hannah said.

What could it be? Nothing remained after all these years. Unless it was a bone?

"It's a bone," Hannah said.

"Stop finding things," Anna said.

"I can't help it. I just put my hand down and it was there. It isn't a human bone. It's too little."

Yes, it would be very small. That didn't mean it wasn't important.

"Did you say it wasn't important?" Hannah said.

"No," Anna said.

Hannah slowly rolled it back and forth. "Because it is. I just know it."

It was an innocent little critter. And Ildred had let it die.

"It has something to do with Ildred," Hannah said.

Anna didn't want to think about Ildred so she sang the song out loud. "Oo, oo. Oo oo, ga, ga."

"I hate that song," Hannah said.

"Well, I hate being in here." Anna sang louder. "Oo, oo. Oo, oo, ga, ga."

Hannah closed her fist protectively around the bone.

Time passed. For the twins, these hours in the darkness felt like forever. Finally the front door opened.

"Hannah Anna! We're back!" Mrs. Zimmer called.

"You took too long in the fabric store. Marcus will be here in forty-five minutes." Selena ran up the stairs and into her room. She tossed two red bags on her bed.

"Selena!" voices wailed from inside the closet.

She backed away from her frightened reflection.

"Please, Selena. Open the door."

Then Selena realized it was only her sisters. "Ha, ha, very funny."

"It isn't a trick. We're stuck."

Selena's thoughts were a swirl of nervous excitement as she hurried into the bathroom to wash her face.

After the twins kicked at the door, Mrs. Zimmer heard the thumping and came upstairs. "What's going on?"

"The twins are in my closet playing another trick on me, which is so not funny because Marcus will be here soon," Selena called from the bathroom.

It took Mr. Zimmer, Mrs. Zimmer, a wrench, and a

screwdriver to pry open the door. The moment it swung clear, Anna raced out and hugged her parents. Hannah carefully shut the door with the fist that was still clenched around the tiny bone.

"Girls, I want to talk to you." Mrs. Zimmer did have a stern voice—when the subject was Selena.

The twins followed their mother downstairs. They stood in front of the hall tree mirror. The crack separated their faces.

"Hannah Anna, stop trying to scare Selena."

"I wasn't," Anna said.

"Then why were you hiding in her closet?" Mrs. Zimmer said.

Hannah held out her fist. "We found something very important. A terrible thing happened in the closet. We should have realized on the first day when Selena felt it."

"Stop talking nonsense. Just promise me you won't bother Selena again."

"No, Mom, listen," Hannah said.

Did she really think her mother would?

"I found a tiny bone." Hannah opened her fist.

Mrs. Zimmer leaned forward to examine it. "That's not a bone. It's a button."

A button?

"It might be made of bone. It looks old. It must have come from someone's fancy dress."

"A button?" Hannah was puzzled. "Could something bad happen to a dress?"

"Of course. If someone ripped it," Mrs. Zimmer said.

No! No one should care about a ripped dress.

"Then who carved their name in the door?" Hannah said.

"What name?" Mrs. Zimmer said.

"Something evil, right, Anna?" Hannah said.

Anna shrugged. "It's just some scratches."

"No, it isn't. You were as scared as I was," Hannah said.

"Of course. You were stuck," Mrs. Zimmer said.

"It's more than that. Something terrible happened in there," Hannah said.

Suddenly three loud thumps echoed from somewhere upstairs.

WHAM WHAM WHAM!

No one spoke.

"It's coming from inside the closet," Hannah whispered.

WHAM WHAM WHAM!

Slowly Hannah climbed the stairs. Mrs. Zimmer and Anna followed. Selena poked her head out of the bathroom.

The door to Selena's room was shut. When the sound came again, the door quivered. *WHAM WHAM WHAM!*

Hannah squeezed the button so tightly that her hand hurt.

The door swung open. They all drew in their breath.

Out came Mr. Zimmer. He wiped a few beads of sweat off his brow with his forearm because his right hand held a hammer.

"Dad's the monster." Anna laughed with relief.

"He's only dangerous when he plays his music too loud," Mrs. Zimmer said.

"What were you doing?" Hannah said.

"Putting in a hook and eye so no one forgets and goes in there."

"With a hammer?" Hannah said.

"I couldn't find the drill." Mr. Zimmer smiled sheepishly.

"There's an explanation for everything. You see, Hannah?" Mrs. Zimmer said.

Hannah saw that her family believed she was foolish. She threw the button onto the floor and walked into her bedroom.

She lay on her bed and thought Anna was right. She did have too much imagination. It used to be fun to think things. Only now she couldn't seem to stop and the things she thought were alarming. She remembered how when they were in the closet, she imagined someone else was there too.

Yes.

Then she remembered how she and Anna had fought. How that felt just as scary as the closet.

Why did she care about Anna? Did Anna care about her?

Hannah jumped down from her bed and walked determinedly over to the dresser. She picked up the book that Georgia had given Anna. Its cover was like Selena's red shopping bags. Anna was always urging Hannah to read it because all the other girls had. Hannah hadn't cared about fitting in with the other kids—until now. She took a deep breath and opened it to the first page.

Hannah didn't like the book. It was easy to see why. It didn't have any adventures. It was just girls making cruel comments about clothes. She should have put down the book. Instead she turned a page.

No.

She was so close to understanding. If only she would listen.

Listen.

She shut the book. "Anna?"

It wasn't her sister who had spoken to her.

The doorbell rang.

"That's Marcus!" Selena shouted. "Somebody let him in. I'm not ready, and it's all Hannah's fault."

Mr. Zimmer opened the front door.

Marcus wasn't smiling his famous gap-toothed smile. He squirmed uneasily, especially when Mr. Zimmer tried to shake his hand with a hammer.

"I'm Selena's dad. She'll be right down. Come on in." Mr. Zimmer gestured with his hammer. "Always something to fix in an old house."

"Especially *this* house," Marcus said.

"What about this house?" Mr. Zimmer said.

"Nothing. Nobody believes that anymore, about the green eyes."

Then why did the young man shift from foot to foot and inch closer to the door?

"Is Selena coming?" Marcus said.

"What about the green eyes?" Mr. Zimmer asked.

Marcus shrugged. "When we were kids, we'd come here on Halloween and watch for them. Until we got bored and threw rocks at the house." He laughed.

So he was one of those boys. Well, well, well . . .

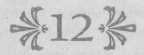

Selena clattered down the stairs in boots with high heels. Marcus grabbed her hand and pulled her out of the house. He was bold now, especially after he got in his car and locked the doors.

At the end of the driveway, a strange wind swirled a tornado of dead leaves. He backed the car right through them. Gravel spit from under the wheels as the car turned onto Hemlock Road. Marcus and Selena laughed as they sped away, as if they knew they couldn't be followed.

That didn't matter. Sooner or later the lovebirds would have to come back.

The sun sank behind the house. Shadows spread across the yard. Cats slunk under the bushes just beyond the property line, where no one could bother them.

The front door opened. Mrs. Zimmer carried a tray. "Bring a cloth," she said.

Mr. Zimmer brought out something white. "This one?"

"Oh no. That's Mrs. Mason's silk." She took it away from him and carefully folded it. The edge blew up in her face. Ha!

After a few minutes, she came back out with an old purple sheet. Anna brought a stack of plates.

"Where's Hannah?" Mr. Zimmer said.

Anna didn't know. She thought how strange it was that she didn't. "I better go get her." She hurried back inside.

"I hope Hannah isn't still upset about the closet. Where does she get these ideas?" Mrs. Zimmer said.

"Kids probably talk at school. They like to think old places are haunted."

"That's ridiculous."

Was it?

After the twins came out, Mrs. Zimmer smiled at Hannah.

"I thought we should have a picnic supper. We hardly ever spend time in the yard. We need to appreciate the good things about living here."

She spread the cloth on the grass. The family sat cross-legged around the food. The house loomed above them. Its dark wood seemed especially gloomy in contrast to the mauve twilight sky. Hannah tried to tell herself that didn't mean anything except that it was getting dark.

The Zimmers ate a strange meal. They each took a paper-thin circle of bread like a pancake. They spooned on a little salad. Then they wrapped the circle in a long tube and ate it with their fingers. They said it was delicious. That was their dinner? Where was the meat? Where were the potatoes? Maybe the Zimmers were as poor as other families used to be.

"Isn't it wonderful to be outside?" Mrs. Zimmer said.

"Sure is," Mr. Zimmer said.

"We could never have done this in Brooklyn," Mrs. Zimmer said.

Hannah sighed at the mention of that other place.

"Just look at all those stars," Mr. Zimmer said.

"The sky had hardly any stars in Brooklyn," Mrs. Zimmer said.

"There's always the same number. Sometimes you just can't see them," Hannah said.

She was right. Things really were there, even when they were unable to be seen.

"Such smart girls we have," Mr. Zimmer said.

"Yes. Too smart to believe silly stories about ghosts," Mrs. Zimmer said.

"Or green eyes," Mr. Zimmer said.

"Did you hear about green eyes too?" Hannah said.

"No," Mrs. Zimmer said firmly.

"A boy on the school bus talked about them," Hannah said.

"Georgia says don't believe anything he says. He likes to hear himself talk."

Just like that Georgia.

Anna spotted the gray cat by the chokeberry bush. "There's Mr. Muffin. He cleaned himself up. Come on, Hannah." She skipped across the grass toward it.

Somehow Mr. Murderer had managed to rid his fur of the muck.

All the Zimmers went over to where the cat sat licking his paw. Mr. Zimmer brought a pink bit of fish. He crouched down and held out his offering. Of course, people always worshipped the cruel ones.

The cat sniffed as if considering whether it was worthy. Then he gobbled it up.

"Can we keep him?" Anna said. "It would make Hannah happy."

"Would it?" Mrs. Zimmer said.

Hannah nodded. She actually thought that the cat would be a friend.

What about the others in the house? What about the innocent critters? Didn't Hannah care about them anymore?

No. She knelt down and let the cat lick her fingers. "He's such a pretty kitty."

A wind came up from nowhere. A wind not on any weatherman's map. The branches of the hemlock trees whipped from side to side. The paper plates danced around the yard. The purple cloth billowed up as if someone stood under it. If it had been white, would they have thought they were seeing a ghost?

"We should go in," Mrs. Zimmer said.

"Feels like a storm's coming," Mr. Zimmer said.

Oh yes, a storm was coming.

"Poor Mr. Muffin. I better bring him too." When Anna tried to pick up the cat, something rubbed his fur the wrong way. The cat yowled. He bared his teeth and claws—the weapons cats hid under soft fur. Anna dropped him. He ran back across the property line.

The wind kept blowing. It chased the Zimmers into the house. All except Selena—and that boy who threw rocks. They had yet to return.

When they did, would the boy see the green eyes? Even though the cat was gone, the anger remained.

Someone was behind the front-door window.

It was Hannah, watching the branches of the hemlock tree battle the wind. Then she turned away and went back to the red-shopping-bag book.

Now there was nothing to do except patrol the edge of the road. Back and forth, back and forth. Watching for the boy. Waiting for the chance to have a little fun.

A car came into the driveway. It stopped. The lights went dark. The car was quiet. No one got out. Of course, they would stay inside, with the doors locked, doing what teenagers did in dark cars. The lovebirds paid no attention to the house on Hemlock Road. Marcus didn't remember throwing rocks. Selena wasn't thinking about her closet.

Maybe they could forget. But others couldn't. Others wouldn't. Ever.

Around and around the car. Dead leaves from last winter rattled against the rear windshield.

"What was that?" Selena said.

"Nothing." Marcus kept his lips close to her face.

A cold breath blew across her cheek. "That tickles."

Selena thought his kiss made the hairs rise along the back of her neck.

Now someone else was watching the dark car. Someone else paced back and forth, wondering what to do about the pretty girl and the thoughtless boy. That person decided enough was enough. The porch light blinked on and off many times.

"What's that?" Marcus said nervously.

Selena laughed. This time she knew what made the electricity flicker. "Just my dad. I better go."

Reluctantly they got out of the car and ambled toward the house. They stopped right at the edge of the darkness. They thought they would be safe as long as they stayed out of the yellow circle of light.

They kissed again. They were just as single-minded as the moths that bumped against the bulb hanging over the front door.

Suddenly all the bats soared out of the attic. It was time for them to hunt. As they flapped after the moths, the bats flew straight at the humans who stood in their way.

Selena screamed as loud and as long as the scream that had started in her closet.

Did her boyfriend comfort her? No. He stumbled back to his car so fast he slipped and fell on the driveway. He scraped his hand on the rocks just like the ones boys had thrown at the green eyes. Ha!

Oh, it was a grand night for feasting. All the critters had their fill. Selena sat on the sofa and wailed about how the bats attacked just as Marcus was about to ask her for another date. Ha! Now that coward wouldn't dare come back to the house on Hemlock Road. Let Selena learn how it felt to be unloved. Let the pretty one suffer for a change.

Was Hannah enjoying her older sister's misery? No. She was upstairs lying on Anna's bed. Hannah held the red-shopping-bag book. Anna held the flashlight. Sometimes they rolled their eyes at a sentence. But they didn't stop reading until they fell asleep. The book dropped and landed on its back on the floor. No one else wanted to read about clothes. A wind blew the cover shut.

Sunday wasn't a day of rest. Mrs. Zimmer went on a rampage after she found a ragged hole in the middle of the piece of white silk. What was she so angry about? A mouse had only borrowed a little bit of fabric to make a nest for her babies. Mrs. Zimmer pulled fabric off the shelves until she found a fluffy ball of threads. Inside slept six tiny babies too young to run away. Mrs. Zimmer scooped them onto a dustpan and tossed them out in the backyard.

Where was Hannah? She could save the babies. At least she could put them someplace where the cats wouldn't get them. Unfortunately she didn't care about any of the critters. She and Anna were cleaning their room— to get ready for Georgia.

Anna crammed all the books back on the shelves except the red-shopping-bag book. Then she handed Hannah a different top with the name of a store written on it. Anna thought everything would be wonderful if only Georgia liked Hannah.

All this fussing made Hannah nervous. "If you say she actually likes me, then why do I have to change?"

"She does like *you*. Only she's tired of your Park Slope shirt."

Soon a midnight-blue van stopped in the driveway. Georgia got out. She thought the house looked creepier than it did from the bus. That didn't scare her. Nothing did.

As she ran up the front steps to the porch, Anna peeked out through the glass.

Georgia gasped. "Oh no! I see a ghost!" She pointed a trembling finger at the window and pretended to faint. Of course Anna laughed like this was the funniest thing ever. She even called to Hannah, "Come see what Georgia's doing."

Hannah's face appeared in the window. She chuckled too—even though she knew how horrible it felt to be laughed at.

The moment Georgia saw Hannah, she stood up and came inside. "Come on, Anna. Let's go to your room to do our homework."

"Hannah has the same assignment," Anna said.

"She has to do a character questionnaire?" Georgia said.

"Yes. And I'm having trouble with it," Hannah said.

"It should be easy for her—she's such a character," Georgia said.

Anna and Hannah laughed like Georgia was only teasing. Anyone who could read thoughts knew she wasn't.

"I can't write about the character I wanted to. Wilbur from *Charlotte's Web* is a pig," Hannah said.

"So?" Georgia said.

"Miz D won't let us mention any food because her doctor said she had to lose fifty pounds or else."

"You could do Charlotte," Anna said.

"Miz D is so hungry she would probably eat a spider," Hannah said.

Anna laughed.

Georgia didn't. She only wanted Anna to enjoy *her* jokes. "Your sister shouldn't make fun of her teacher. Let's get started. Is your room upstairs?"

Georgia led the way. The door to Selena's room slowly opened. Perhaps Georgia might enjoy spending time in the closet? She took a step toward the door.

Anna grabbed her arm and led her down the hall to the twins' room.

"Bunk beds?" Georgia clapped her hands against her cheeks in horror.

"What's wrong with them?" Anna said.

"Aren't you too old for that?" Georgia said.

"There isn't much space," Hannah said.

"You'd have more room if you got rid of those shelves," Georgia said.

That was a terrible idea. The door banged shut behind her. Everybody jumped.

"Must have been the wind," Anna said.

Hannah looked around the room and wondered. Had something gone out—or come in?

Georgia sat down at Hannah's desk. From her book bag, she took a piece of paper with the title "Character Questionnaire." There were lots of blanks to fill in. Georgia patted the chair next to hers and smiled at Anna. "I brought my nail polish. I'll give you a manicure when we're done."

Anna made Hannah sit closer to Georgia.

Hannah tried to be friendly. "What character did you pick, Georgia?"

"Myself," Georgia said.

"Don't you have to do a character from a book?" Hannah said.

"I'm going to be such a famous designer, I'll be in lots of books."

"Really?" Hannah said.

"Tell your sister that I'm kidding." Georgia selected a purple pen and wrote on her paper in beautiful loopy penmanship. Anna wrote too.

Hannah didn't. Oh, it was horrible to be stuck—especially when others glided along without a care in the world.

Georgia smirked at Hannah's blank paper. She was glad she and Anna would finish first. Then they could ditch Hannah and put pretty colors on their fingernails.

Hannah put her pencil against the paper, even though she still had no idea what to write. She wanted to remember the character in that red-shopping-bag book. She thought that might make Georgia like her.

Then she noticed the door to her own closet move just an inch. Uninvited thoughts flooded her brain. Why hadn't anything happened in this closet? What was special about Selena's closet? What *had* happened there? Why was the name carved in the door? Whose name was it?

Hannah's pencil moved across the paper. Her first mark was a slash, like the carving in the door. The second was bent. The third had a mouth. The fourth had legs. The fifth had more slashes. And the sixth was another mouth, only it was twisted into a scream.

ILDRED

14

"I'm done," Georgia crowed as she snapped the cap back on her pen. She leaned over to read what Hannah had written. "What kind of character is that?"

Anna stood up to see. She quickly flipped over Hannah's piece of paper. "Stop kidding around," she said fiercely.

"I'm not." Hannah turned the paper over and kept writing.

"Is your sister crazy?" Georgia said.

"No," Anna said. Anna knew she couldn't answer any more questions. "Come on, Georgia. Let's go outside to do our nails."

Anna and Georgia went downstairs.

"My friend Kyla who's in your sister's class says she acts like she's from another planet. And that planet isn't even in our solar system." Georgia's voice trailed away.

Hannah ignored her and everyone else as she filled in the blanks with what she *thought* was true.

> Name: ILDRED
> Book: Murder
> Strengths: Viciousness
> Flaws: Envy
> Favorite food: Torment
> Family: None
> Place of residence: The house on Hemlock
>   Road
> Hangouts: The closet

Hannah was wrong. Ildred didn't hang out in the closet. Or even the place beyond the house. Ildred didn't haunt the scenes of its crimes. Ildred had left nearly eighty years ago.

Others were stuck. Others could never leave. No matter what they did or how they tried.

Being stuck wasn't quite so painful anymore. Hannah was listening now. At least, she was trying to. Maybe one day she really would hear. A girl like Hannah might be able to understand. If Anna would just leave Hannah alone.

Anna was right about one thing: Hannah should give her teacher a different character questionnaire. Miz D didn't need to read the lies Hannah had written about Ildred.

The twins argued about that until they got on the bus the next morning. Anna sat with Georgia. Hannah sat with the little children in the front, as far away from teasing as possible. The bus drove off and no one could know what happened during the day. One thing was certain. Hannah would be miserable.

Right after the twins returned home, an orange car shaped like a big bug drove into the driveway. It even had big black spots. A large woman got out and stared at the house. She had black frizzy hair. Pink plastic giraffes dangled from her ears. Her blue dress was the size of a tent. She pressed one hand over her heart. The other hand clutched a plastic bag of celery sticks.

"It *is* the house," she said.

Hannah was shocked to see Miz D standing in the yard. Hannah didn't think she was in so much trouble at school that her teacher would come to the house. She bravely opened the front door and came out.

Then the most amazing thing happened. Miz D lurched toward Hannah and smothered her in a hug.

"Oh, Hannah, you poor little cupcake. You're such a brave girl. I had no idea."

Miz D released her for a moment, only to hug her again. "I pride myself on being sensitive to my students. But I let you down."

"That's okay." Hannah squirmed out from under her teacher's armpit. She wasn't used to being liked by Miz D.

"I should have looked up your address before. It can be helpful to see what the home situation is like—especially when a student can't get along with the others."

What was that supposed to mean? Was she blaming Hannah? Unfortunately Hannah wasn't sticking up for herself. And no one else could.

"I spent *many* nights thinking about you. What would change your negative thoughts? How could I help you get along with the other children and find your place in our happy classroom?"

A breeze toyed with the bottom of the blue tent dress. It was no match for the hot air coming from Miz D's mouth.

"As wise as I am, you had me stumped until you turned in that character questionnaire about . . . Ildred."

Hannah's heart pounded when Miz D whispered the name. "What about it?"

"It lived in the house on Hemlock Road. At first I thought, it couldn't be *that* house. No one would live in such a horrible house. But you do, don't you, my poor little cupcake." Miz D tried to embrace Hannah again.

Hannah stepped aside. "It isn't so bad."

Miz D clapped her hands. "You're taking my advice about improving your attitude. That's wonderful. Don't even *listen* to what people say about this house. It's been years since anyone has seen the green eyes."

"The green eyes?"

"If they ever really did. And nobody patrols the property."

"Patrols?"

"Yes, dear, you know, paces back and forth along the boundary. Like a soldier."

Miz D turned and pointed to the hemlock trees. A branch waved gaily at her. She didn't realize she was being taunted.

"When people see a breeze like that, they think a ghost is pacing. Now it *is* true that a soldier lived on Hemlock Road."

"A soldier?" Hannah's mind seized this information.

"Yes. He was a brave hero in World War One. And then . . ." Miz D paused dramatically. "Tragedy."

Did she know? It was difficult to tell. Her thoughts were battling hunger signals from her stomach.

"So many men suffered from shell shock. They became living ghosts."

"Then there *is* a ghost," Hannah said.

"Oh no," Miz D said.

"You just said there was." Hannah was puzzled.

"I used a metaphor. There's no such thing as ghosts. No, they aren't the problem with the house."

An ominous rumbling sound seemed to come from the depths of the earth. Miz D belched loudly and thumped her chest. "Pardon me. Celery gives me gas. But I won't eat anything else until I lose forty-six more pounds."

"Then what *is* wrong with the house?"

Miz D gestured toward the house with the bag of celery. "I could tell the first time I saw it. Twenty years ago, my college friend Emily brought me here. I had just started teaching in Helton. Emily thought it would be fun to see where her grandmother used to live. Well, let me tell you, it was *not* fun."

"It wasn't?" Hannah said.

Miz D solemnly shook her head. "As I said, I'm very sensitive to feelings. The moment I saw this house, I knew it was responsible for all the tragedies in Emily's family."

Tragedies?

"Alcoholism. Divorce. Families shattered in all sorts of ways."

Those weren't tragedies. *No no no*, the branch waved angrily.

"How could a house cause that?" Hannah said.

"This house is full of hate. Resentment is still rolling off the roof." Miz D waved her arm in a big circle.

If there was hate, other people started it.

"Envy gushes out from the eaves."

Hannah smiled at the exaggerated expression.

Miz D shook her finger. "Never underestimate the evil of envy. Think of the wars we fought just because some people wanted what other people had."

They wanted what had been taken from them. That was natural. That was right. They shouldn't be blamed. It wasn't their fault. It wasn't. It was those other people.

The wind whipped the branches of the hemlock back and forth. Like a father lashing out with his belt. *Hate hate hate.*

Miz D stared at the trees. "It must be a storm. We should go inside."

A branch cracked. It dangled dangerously from the tree.

She turned toward the house and gasped. "Oh my. We can't. Not in there."

"Why not?" Hannah said.

Miz D pointed at the front door.

"Why not?" Hannah said again. "What are you looking at? What do you see?"

What did that teacher see? Her own resentment. Her own envy. Her own hate.

Miz D opened her mouth. She didn't speak; she gasped for air. Her face turned red, and then white, as her large body crumpled to the ground.

❊15❊

now that had never happened before.

People had run away screaming. People had staggered off gasping for breath. People had stood paralyzed. People had slowly backed away shaking their heads no. But nobody had collapsed on the ground like a big balloon that had suddenly lost its hot air.

The branches of the hemlock trees were still.

Was the teacher dead?

Her arm was stretched out on the grass next to the bag of celery sticks. Hannah stared at the arm. It didn't twitch or wriggle. Sometimes not doing anything was the most frightening thing of all. Hannah put her hands over her eyes and screamed.

Everyone came running. Mrs. Zimmer held a piece of maroon cloth and a pair of scissors. Anna carried the cordless phone. So Georgia was there too, in a way, shouting,

"Why is your sister screaming?" until Mrs. Zimmer took the phone away from Anna to call an ambulance.

"Hurry," she told them.

Miz D was still breathing—just barely.

Hannah knelt next to her teacher. She was afraid to touch her. She tentatively untangled the earring caught in Miz D's hair. She wanted to make something right. Even if it was a very small thing.

The siren got closer and closer until the ambulance stopped in the driveway. Two men in white uniforms jumped out. One put a mask over Miz D's face to give her oxygen. The other listened to her heart. Somehow the men lifted Miz D onto a cot. They wheeled her into the back of the ambulance and shut the doors. Everyone watched the ambulance leave. They stared at the road through the hemlock trees for as long as they could still hear the siren.

Then there was silence.

"That was your teacher?" Mrs. Zimmer was worried that Hannah was in trouble at school.

Hannah nodded. Her mind swirled. She was very upset. She shouldn't have been. Miz D wasn't dead. The worst hadn't happened to her.

"It's my fault she came here. I wrote about the house. In the questionnaire." Hannah hid her face in her mother's shirt.

It wasn't Hannah's fault. Plenty of people came to the house on Hemlock Road because they wanted to see something dreadful. And Miz D had.

"She could have had a heart attack anywhere," Mrs. Zimmer said.

Hannah shook her head. "She saw something. Right before she collapsed. I have to go to the hospital."

"I know you're worried about your teacher," Mrs. Zimmer said.

"I have to ask her what she saw," Hannah said.

"You told me her doctor wanted her to lose weight." Anna picked up the bag of celery and showed it to Hannah.

"I have to know what we're living with," Hannah whispered.

Mrs. Zimmer hugged Hannah. She pushed her mother away. "You should want to know too. You should stop pretending there isn't anything wrong."

"There isn't. Your teacher wasn't well. So she had a heart attack." Mrs. Zimmer struggled to keep calm. She thought Hannah was overreacting again. She worried that this was a more serious problem than she thought. "I'll make tea. I'm sure we could all use a cup. Hannah? Anna? Tension tamer tea?"

Anna followed her mother.

Hannah stayed outside. She wanted to see what her teacher had seen.

She stood where Miz D had been standing. She looked where Miz D had been looking. She opened her eyes wide. She squinted. She saw how the shutter dangled from one hinge. She saw the red leaves of the chokeberry bush. She saw that horrible cat skulking along the porch.

"Ildred?" Hannah whispered.

Ildred didn't answer. It never did. It ignored others. It was selfish and cruel.

Still Hannah stared at the house, hoping to see what monstrosity had scared Miz D. Her heart pounded.

She had nothing to fear. No one in the house hated her.

Hannah gasped. What had she seen? There—in the dining room window. A woman with no head and no arms!

Then Hannah smiled at the dressmaker's dummy. She remembered how she and Anna used to play with Beulah Buttons. When a game required an extra character, Beulah had been a teacher, a wizard, and a mermaid. Once Anna had made a head and arms for Beulah. Hannah thought how Anna always tried to fix things that were broken.

Suddenly Hannah very much wanted to see her sister. She ran up along the walk toward the house.

Wait.

Didn't she know that Anna would only make her unhappy? Didn't she know that Anna was probably on the phone, laughing about her with Georgia? Didn't Hannah know who her true friend was?

Wait.

Hannah ran up the steps to the porch. Her feet clomped on the wood. She put her hand on the old brass knob. She didn't turn it. She clung to it for dear life as she stood there, staring at the glass in the door.

Someone was inside, looking out.

❧16❧

Hannah didn't collapse like Miz D. She inched away from the door. Unfortunately she forgot about the steps. She fell, tumbling all the way down to the yard. Then she lay there. She liked feeling the solid ground beneath her. In fact, she dug her fingers in the dirt. She was trying to hang on to the earth.

Why? So what if she had seen someone. That wasn't a bad thing. Or was it? Who knew what had happened to a face, after nearly eighty years.

Mrs. Zimmer glanced out the living room window. When she saw her daughter on the ground, she hurried out of the house. "Hannah, are you all right?"

Anna came outside too. Together they helped Hannah sit up. Hannah stared at the front door with such a strange expression that Mrs. Zimmer asked, "Did you hit your head when you fell?"

"No." Hannah was transfixed.

"Your elbow is scraped. I'll get some ointment." Mrs. Zimmer hugged Hannah and went inside.

"What happened?" Anna said.

"I saw something. Just like Miz D."

"Oh, Hannah." Anna sounded like a disappointed old grandmother.

"In the window. Right there." Hannah stood up and pointed.

"I suppose you saw the green eyes."

Hannah thought for a moment. "Yes. The eyes were green."

"*Your* eyes are green. You saw your reflection. That's all. I'll prove it to you." Anna stood beside Hannah. Now they were both staring at the glass.

The twins no longer looked identical. One had a rumpled shirt. Her hair hung limp. The other had a cute striped top. Her hair had three small braids that Georgia probably had given her that day at recess. However, the twins couldn't see any of this because they couldn't see their reflections.

"Well?" Hannah said.

"The light must be different now," Anna said.

"I saw the face just a minute ago."

"So? Maybe the light was different. Maybe clouds were in front of the sun."

"Or maybe I *did* see the face."

Why was Hannah arguing with Anna? Who cared if

Anna believed her or not? Hannah had seen. So now Hannah must know.

"Know," Hannah said.

Had she understood? Had she?

Hannah came closer to the window again. Her breath fogged the glass.

"Know what?" Anna said.

"I mean, no, I didn't see it," Hannah said.

What? How could she doubt it now?

"You didn't?" Anna said.

"It wasn't the right face," Hannah said.

What did she mean? It was the only face.

"You're not making any sense," Anna said.

"I didn't see the one Miz D told me about," Hannah said as she hurried inside.

She found her mother in the kitchen, rummaging through a box. Mrs. Zimmer held a package of birthday candles and a bottle of salad dressing.

"I can't seem to find the first-aid kit," Mrs. Zimmer said.

Hannah didn't care about that. "Mom, I need to go to the library right now."

Mrs. Zimmer dropped the things back in the box. "Now?"

"Can you drive me?"

Mrs. Zimmer thought of a hundred reasons why Hannah shouldn't go.

Once upon a time, certain girls loved to visit the town

library. It was the one place they could visit. Movies cost too much. But the library was free. Yes, free. Nobody had to pay one single nickel to walk up the wide steps, past the stone lions, and into the beautiful redbrick mansion. *The Story of the Treasure Seekers* had first been discovered at the library.

Maybe someone had donated a new copy? Maybe Hannah could find it and bring it to the house on Hemlock Road?

Hannah wasn't thinking about that wonderful book. She was wondering about the soldier—the one Miz D had called the living ghost.

"Mom, it's important. It's for school."

Mrs. Zimmer sighed. "Can't you use the Internet?"

What kind of net?

Hannah raced upstairs and into her parents' bedroom. She sat down at the desk and turned on the contraption they called the computer, even though no one ever used it for computing. She typed in the words *Helton, Soldier, World War I*. A long list appeared on the screen. Hannah sighed. She thought she would never find out anything this way. She was right.

Selena came home and let the door bang behind her. She spun Anna around and around the living room as she shouted, "I have to tell everybody!"

"What?" Anna said.

Mrs. Zimmer came to see what the commotion was about.

"He found me during lunch," Selena said.

"Who? The janitor?" Anna couldn't share her joke with Hannah. She wasn't there.

"No. Marcus. I thought he was going to ask me to the movies. Only he didn't."

Mrs. Zimmer braced herself for more hysterics.

Selena did scream. "He asked me to the homecoming dance!" She abruptly stopped jumping and ominously held up a finger. "There's one condition. We have to get rid of those disgusting bats."

No!

"All right," Mrs. Zimmer said. "I'd like to exterminate the whole house. I found more mouse poop in the kitchen."

Where was Hannah? She could explain that the critters never did anything wrong. They never murdered anybody. What was Hannah doing? Why was she still upstairs staring at that screen?

The list was gone. Somehow or other she had found a picture of a newspaper article. It was the one on display at the Maplethorpe Library in the case with the guns and the helmet. That photo of the dreamy-eyed soldier had been taken before the war. Before he had been in the trenches. Before he had killed anyone.

HELTON'S HERO RETURNS TODAY

Blah blah blah.

A breeze blew in Hannah's ear. A sleeve rose up from a shirt draped over a chair. The sheet billowed out from the unmade bed. Hannah didn't notice any of this. She kept reading about how bravely Lieutenant Maplethorpe had fought. How he got separated from his unit. How weeks later he was found in a trench sitting next to three dead German soldiers. How he spent ten years in a hospital recovering from mysterious injuries the reporter refused to describe. And how, after that long convalescence, Lieutenant Maplethorpe had been taken to his family's house on Hemlock Road.

17

When Hannah finished reading, she looked at the sleeve of the shirt and wondered if someone was there. "Did you come to this house?" Hannah whispered.

No, not this house.

She read the article again. It didn't mention the address or anything else significant. It had been written ten whole years before the most important story began.

She pushed a button that somehow made the article appear on a piece of paper. She hid that paper in her underwear drawer.

Didn't she realize Mr. Zimmer was calling a company called Pest Control Services? Didn't she care that those people promised to get rid of all the bats one week from Friday? Didn't she care that the bats only had eleven days and eleven nights left to live?

No, all she thought about was Lieutenant Maplethorpe.

Oh, the poor brave soldier. Why wasn't he resting in peace? What had Ildred done to him? When could Hannah go back in the closet to look for more clues? It was too infuriating to read her mind. Even Selena's daydreams about Marcus were more interesting.

The next day Hannah brought a stack of books home from school. They were all about World War I.

Anna followed her into their room. "I have to talk to you."

Hannah wasn't listening to anybody or anything. She read how the assassination of the archduke caused all those countries to go to war.

Anna shut the book. "Georgia is having a makeover party."

"So?" Hannah said.

"So we're invited," Anna said.

"Me too?" Hannah said.

"Yes." Anna was quite proud of persuading Georgia that it would be loads of fun to have Hannah there.

"It's a sleepover. You'll get to know her better. And her friends. Kyla from your class will be there," Anna said.

Hannah thought how Kyla spent the day pretending to have a heart attack whenever she saw Hannah. The substitute teacher, Mr. Ogbert, couldn't control the class like Miz D.

"And she'll get to know you." Anna took the books about World War I. She thought it had been bad enough when Hannah was a nerd. Now she was becoming a weirdo.

Hannah grabbed the books back. The sisters had a tug-of-war. Hannah won.

"Why do you want to read these?" Anna said.

"Why do you want me to go to Georgia's party?"

"I want you to have fun. With me." Anna didn't say the rest of her thought. How she worried about Hannah and missed her—the way Hannah used to be.

Hannah was too busy planning to even try to understand Anna. If Anna was with Georgia, and the rest of her family left, then Hannah could go in Selena's closet and search for more clues about what had happened to her soldier.

The week passed. The bats had only seven days left. And all Hannah had done was read her books about World War I. What did she learn? That war was senseless. People died for no good reason.

There weren't any books written that could change that.

On Saturday, Anna went to Georgia's. Hannah hardly said good-bye. The rest of the Zimmers were going shopping. They always thought they needed to buy something, when what they really wanted was to escape the house.

"Wouldn't you like to come?" Mr. Zimmer felt sorry that Hannah was left out.

"It can't be good for you to stay home alone." Mrs. Zimmer thought that Hannah was still upset about her teacher.

Hannah smiled. She knew she wouldn't be alone.

"You could help me pick out my dress for the dance," Selena said.

"I have homework," Hannah said.

The Zimmers got in the silver car. The hemlock branches waved them away.

Hurry, hurry.

This might be the last chance to tell Hannah she had to save the bats.

Listen.

"Hello? Are you there?"

Of course. Didn't she know it was impossible to leave?

"You are there." She stood in the hall and looked toward the top of the window in the front door. That was where she thought Miz D had seen the soldier's face. She saw nothing. She wished she could ask Miz D. Her teacher still wasn't allowed any visitors.

"I'm going in the closet."

No.

Hannah heard the word *go*. She climbed the stairs and entered Selena's room. As usual, clothes were everywhere. As she reached up to undo the hook, a purple scarf floated in the air and covered her face.

"Don't you want me to go in there?"

No.

"I understand," she said. But she didn't.

"Something very bad happened to you in there. Were you killed in there? Was it Ildred?" She whispered the last word.

She twisted the scarf nervously as she waited for an answer.

The attic.

"Trick? What kind of trick?"

Hannah was frustrated. She wasn't the only one.

"I know you want to tell me something. I just don't know what. I know. I'll have a séance."

She had read about one in a book. She thought she knew what to do. She cleared the clothes away from the closet. When she had a nice bare space, she carefully folded the scarf and put it in the center. She got the sheet of paper with the newspaper article and put it next to the scarf. She looked everywhere for candles. All she could find were the three on Selena's dresser. One was a pair of red lips, one was a cupcake, and one was a big square yellow sponge with a face. It seemed to be wearing blue shorts.

She lit the candles and sat cross-legged next to the display. She held her hands with palms up and moaned in a low voice, "Lootennannt Maapullthorrp."

When people speak to the dead, why do they make their voices sound like sick cows?

"I know you're here. I feel your presence in this room. Speak to me, brave soldier."

Was it brave to kill? A wind slid the paper under the dresser. Ha!

"Maybe you can't speak. Can you thump?"

Well, why not? If she wanted thumps, let her have them. Maybe then she could understand. If only something in the attic could be pounded against the floor. The only things up there were the sleeping bats.

"Where are you? Did you leave? What happened?" Hannah called.

Nothing in the parents' bedroom either. Nothing that a small breeze could knock over. No way to make a loud noise. Hannah would just have to concentrate.

Back in Selena's room, Hannah had stood up. She had retrieved the piece of paper and was clutching it to her chest.

Bats.

"I think I heard you. Say it again?"

BATS!

"Cats?"

What was the matter with her? She must not be trying. She had filled her head with nonsense about that soldier and now she would never hear. Never never never. And all the bats would die.

Die.

"Eye?"

It was hopeless.

"Cat's-eye. I know. That's a kind of a stone. Maybe you had one that was really valuable and someone tried to steal it from you but you wanted to give it to your fiancé so you fought the thief until—"

A breeze blew out her stupid candles.

She buried her face in her hands.

"I'm sorry. I'm trying to understand. Only I just can't."

She was sorry. And she was very upset.

It was wrong to be angry. Especially with her. Friends should forgive friends.

"Should I try again?"

The breeze blew on her hand. With trembling fingers, she relit the candles.

Then she shut her eyes.

That was better. One darkness could meet another. Let the real world go away. Just listen.

Listen.

"I'm listening," she whispered.

She was. She really was.

THUMP.

Oh no.

"I heard it." She clapped her hands excitedly and shut her eyes again. "I don't know what it means. Is one thump yes? Or no?"

THUMP THUMP THUMP THUMP THUMP.

It was too late.

"Tell me."

Footsteps ran up the stairs. The door to the bedroom opened. There was a gasp, then more thumps. Three big puffs of air blew out the candles.

Selena wailed, "Mom! Hannah is in my room *again!*"

Caught. No way to escape. No way to explain. The sister screamed: Why do you keep going where you're not wanted? Look what she's done to my things. She's cut up all my dresses. Why would you do that? What's the matter with you, anyway?

Maybe then she would know how it felt to lose something. How it felt to suffer. Why should she have everything? Even the cat liked her better. The only one who didn't was the mouse that limped. Poor Whiskers. That was why she let the cat kill him in her closet. She could have saved him. But she didn't. She only cared about her dresses. She would never save anybody. She would let others die too. She was a terrible horrible selfish monster. . . .

The mother came in. And the father. Clomping up the steps. Taking off his belt.

No, this time it was the Zimmers, hurrying to see what happened to their precious darling.

Selena pointed at the floor. "Look what Hannah did."

"What's going on up here?" Mr. Zimmer said.

"Is this why you didn't want to go to the mall?" Mrs. Zimmer said.

Don't just stand there, Hannah. Run. Don't let them take away your things. If you hurry, you can hide some. Just like the precious thing in the attic. Run, Hannah, run.

Hannah didn't. She stood up and slowly folded the piece of paper.

"She ruined my special candles," Selena said.

"SpongeBob is special to you?" Hannah said.

"My friends gave them to me before I moved. You wouldn't understand. You don't have any friends," Selena said.

"Yes, I do," Hannah said.

"Name one," Selena said.

Hannah couldn't. She didn't know the name. All she thought about was the soldier.

"You have to pay me for the candles you ruined," Selena said.

"You never pay for what *you* ruin," Hannah said.

"What's the matter with you girls? You never used to fight so much," Mrs. Zimmer said.

"It's because of this house." Hannah held out the piece of paper. "Something happened to this soldier here."

Mrs. Zimmer wouldn't look. She thought she couldn't stand it here one more minute. "You know we can't move until the new house is ready." She turned on her husband. "And your father refuses to call the contractor."

"I do call him. He never calls me back," Mr. Zimmer said.

"He walks all over you just like everybody else does," Mrs. Zimmer said.

"What's that supposed to mean?" Mr. Zimmer said, even though he knew she meant he was weak. He hated being told that.

Mrs. Zimmer also hated—more things than could be named.

Hannah was scared to see her parents acting like this. "It *is* the house. Can't you see that? Now *you're* fighting. And you never used to fight either."

"Don't blame the house. *You're* the one who's acting crazy," Selena said.

Mr. and Mrs. Zimmer looked at Hannah and wondered what was going on inside her head.

Hannah recognized the expression on her parents' faces. It was the one the children at school got when they were thinking something was wrong with her.

She ran into her room and slammed the door.

"You owe me money!" Selena shouted after her.

The house was quiet now, although the walls still seemed to quiver from all the yelling. There was a fresh outburst when Mr. Zimmer made the mistake of asking about dinner. Apparently there wouldn't be any that night—except of course for the mice and the bats. And for

Anna, who was spending the night with Georgia and her friends. What kind of food would they be eating?

Hannah got her book. Books could be so comforting—unless they described shell-shocked soldiers. The book said many of the men who came back from the war would just sit and stare at nothing.

Not all of them did. One paced back and forth, as if he were still in a trench, still in the war, even though it had been nearly twenty years since he had been attacked by Germans. His back bent. His hair got gray. His ditch got deeper. He kept fighting his war against a mother in a vegetable garden and two girls hanging their father's shirts on the clothesline.

Best not to think about that.

A breeze turned the page. Hannah didn't turn it back. She shut the book and put it on her desk.

"Poor Lieutenant Maplethorpe," she said.

After her mother came in and said good night, Hannah put on the enormous T-shirt she wore instead of a proper nightgown. She put her foot on the bottom rung of the ladder. She paused in midair when she saw Anna's empty bed. She thought how disconnected she felt. This was the first night in her entire life she would be without Anna.

Why didn't Hannah remember she wasn't alone?

A breath tickled her cheek. She slowly touched the place.

"Are you here?" she whispered.

Yes.

"I almost heard you before. Then Selena came."

Sisters spoiled everything.

"It's quiet now. Try again."

Bats.

"I'm sorry, I can't quite hear. Can you be louder?"

No.

"Know?" She didn't understand. And yet she did. "Oh. It isn't hearing. It's knowing. Like how I know what Anna's thinking."

Her lip quivered. "Like how I used to know."

She thought that she didn't understand Anna at all anymore—not even when Anna actually spoke.

Bats bats bats. Bats in the attic. Save the bats. Don't let them be killed. Do something.

Hannah wasn't listening anymore.

She sat on the edge of Anna's bed. She picked up the pillow and hugged it. It smelled like something Hannah recognized as lip smackers. Whatever that was, it reminded her of Georgia. She quickly dropped the pillow back on Anna's bed.

She sat there, longing for her sister, as darkness settled around the house.

Did she feel lonely enough to understand? Did she know what it would be like to be left behind? Without even the comfort of the critters? Didn't she care?

No.

It would be better to talk to the bats. Better join their dance. There were only six nights left.

19

The next morning Hannah didn't get dressed or comb her hair or eat breakfast. She was too busy waiting for Anna to come back. All Hannah could think was that Anna should have been home by now. Only Anna wasn't.

At first Hannah waited in the living room. She got tired of jumping up to look out the window every time a car passed by. So she sat on the front porch and plucked the leaves off the chokeberry bush. She couldn't see if Georgia's van was coming around the corner. The hemlock trees were in the way. So Hannah went to the edge of the yard and stood next to the hemlock trees.

Their branches waved, *shush, shush, shush.*

Hannah wasn't listening. As she paced back and forth under the trees, she remembered that the purpose of Georgia's party was to do makeovers. What sort of girl would Anna be when she got back?

A car zipped past. A stone spurted from the wheel. It almost hit Hannah's leg. She didn't care. She kept walking much too close to the edge. How long could she keep this up? Some had done it for nearly eighty years.

Mrs. Zimmer came out of the house. She was worried too—about Hannah.

"Why don't you come in and have breakfast?"

Hannah shook her head. She didn't want food.

"Anna just called. They're going to the movies. They won't be back until five."

"Five?" Hannah thought that sounded like forever. It wasn't, of course. She should have known that.

Mrs. Zimmer stroked the hair back from Hannah's face. "Come inside. Have a shower. When was the last time you washed your hair?"

Hannah rolled her eyes, but she let her mother walk her back toward the house on Hemlock Road.

"You'll feel better if you do. You can use that ginger shampoo that makes your scalp tingle."

Did it? Or did something else electrify the top of Hannah's head? She couldn't be sure.

She did think the shampoo smelled good. Her mother was right. Being clean did make Hannah happier. If only others were still able to feel things like that.

The bathroom mirror was fogged with steam. Hannah wiped it with the sleeve of her bathrobe. She combed her wet hair. It looked longer and darker than it usually did. She was thinking how Anna would probably come home with the rest of her hair all in little braids. They might even have little plastic beads stuck on the ends so that Anna would rattle every time she tossed her head.

Hannah was glad not to be made over like that. She draped half of her hair in front of her right shoulder and the other half in front of her left. She tried to make the ends curl. They were as straight as ever.

Then she leaned closer to the mirror.

The long, wet hair reminded her. She took a step back. She slipped on the damp floor. She gripped the edge of the sink and leaned forward again to stare at the green eyes in the mirror.

Whose eyes were they?

She stroked the wet hair along her face.

The day Miz D collapsed, the day Hannah tried to see what her teacher had seen, Hannah had expected a soldier's face. She had been so certain he was the ghost.

Only now she knew he wasn't.

Now she remembered what she had seen.

A girl with green eyes and long, wet hair.

20

Yes, Hannah knew what she had seen.

She kept staring at the green eyes. She leaned closer. Her breath fogged the mirror. Still the eyes in the mirror burned. There was so much to say.

"Who are you?" Hannah whispered.

Maybe now she could understand everything. Or at least enough to save the bats.

Please listen. Can you hear? Do you know?

Now the mirror showed just Hannah's eyes, confused and a little bit frightened.

She didn't need to be afraid.

"I'm sorry. I still don't understand," Hannah whispered.

Someone knocked loudly on the door. Hannah jumped.

"You know there's only one bathroom in this house,"

Selena said. "Mom and Dad are taking us to the movies. And this time you *have* to come."

After a flurry of getting ready, including a desperate search for Selena's missing shoe, the family went off in the silver car.

Yes, some were left behind again. But the Zimmers would bring Hannah back. They had to.

Anna was with them when they returned. Anna did have dozens of braids tipped with colorful beads that clacked when she tossed her head. She had a circular piece of shiny plastic that played loud music. She had a million stories about how much fun she had had with Georgia and the other girls. If only she had stayed there.

That night, Anna kept talking about why Hannah should make friends with Kyla because she was so funny.

Hannah didn't need Kyla. Hannah had a friend.

Hannah. Are you listening?

Anna spoke. "I know I'm talking a lot. But compared to Georgia's, this house seems so dead."

Dead?

"You really should have come."

Hannah didn't answer. She was asleep.

The pest-control people were coming on Friday. Selena was counting the days. Why wasn't Hannah?

On Monday Hannah came home from school. Her face was pale. Her eyes were red. She couldn't answer when her mother asked her what was wrong. Anna had to say that Miz D had died.

Now Hannah thought of nothing else except her poor

teacher. That death made Hannah so sad—and scared. She too had seen the face.

On Wednesday there would be a memorial at the school. All the students would attend. The room would be full of people, all saying how wonderful Miz D was and how sorry they were. Yes, everybody was sorry *she* was gone.

Once upon a time, there had been another funeral on a rainy day so dark it might as well have been night.

The mother and the father were in black clothes. The sister wasn't. She wore a lavender dress. It was the only one that hadn't been ruined. It hadn't been hanging in the closet when the other dresses were cut up. The mother made the sister wear a black ribbon. Her sleeve flounced over it.

The rain beat at the dying leaves and knocked them off the trees.

The father, the mother, and the sister got in the old flivver. As usual, it didn't want to start. It was always breaking down.

The mother was agitated. She worried about being late.

The father said, *They won't begin the service without us.*

The sister said nothing.

The engine whirred and whirred.

Then the father yelled, *Didn't I tell you both not to go over there? Didn't I say to stay in our yard?*

The sister nodded and smoothed her dress. *Yes, Father.*

She always pretended to be the good daughter. But she wasn't. She just never got caught.

The engine roared to life. The old flivver backed out of the driveway. The father, the mother, and the sister left.

No one else could.

Was the running board too slippery? Surely the old car wasn't too fast.

The father had said, *Stay in the yard*. The father must be obeyed even though it was too late to change anything.

There would be no leaving. Did it matter why?

The family came back that day. One week later they left again. They didn't say good-bye. And they never returned.

But Hannah would.

A different car drove into the driveway. It wasn't the flivver or the Zimmers' silver car. It was red.

The doors opened. Three people got out: Hannah, Anna, and a woman dressed in a dark gray suit. She was medium height, with stylish light-brown hair and glasses. She was a stranger, and yet there was something suspiciously familiar about her.

Mrs. Zimmer came out on the front porch.

"This is Miz D's college friend. She was at the memorial," Hannah said.

"I'm Emily Stryder." The woman held out her hand for Mrs. Zimmer to shake.

"Her grandmother used to live in the house," Hannah said.

"I wanted to see it. I couldn't believe it hadn't been torn down," Emily said.

So many people had come and gone over the years. So

many people, with nothing to distinguish them. Even their screams sounded alike—after all these years.

"It is pretty old," Mrs. Zimmer said.

Emily walked across the yard. "The girls told me Tina had her heart attack right here." She got out a handkerchief and blew her nose.

"We're so sorry," Mrs. Zimmer said.

"Her heart was bad. Had been for years," Emily said.

"You see?" Anna nudged Hannah.

Hannah ignored her and moved closer to Emily. "Can I ask you something?"

"Yes?" Emily said.

"Did your grandmother ever tell you about anything unusual that happened in the house?" Hannah said.

"You must have heard the stories about the green eyes." Emily smiled like she wanted to pat Hannah on the head. "Old houses are full of strange noises and dark corners. They aren't haunted. They're just falling apart."

"That's what I've been telling her." Mrs. Zimmer did pat Hannah on the head.

Hannah shook off her mother's hand. "It isn't just falling apart. I saw the eyes."

"I'm sure you thought you did," Emily said.

Then Hannah remembered. "I can prove it. There's something I can show you. Upstairs. In the closet."

Emily thought the quickest way to exit was to look at whatever Hannah wanted to show her. "All right."

Hannah led the way. Emily frowned at the unpacked

boxes in the hall and the fabric strewn about the dining room. Selena's room was even messier.

"And I thought my daughter was bad. Is this your room, Hannah?" Emily said.

"It's our sister Selena's. The day we moved in, she felt something strange in her closet. So later Anna and I went in. And the door got stuck."

"It was a humid day," Mrs. Zimmer said.

Hannah lifted the hook and opened the closet door.

Could the grown-ups explain the rotten smell of anger that never went away? Of course not. They just tried to breathe through their mouths.

"There. Carved in the wood. Can you see?" Hannah pointed at the letters.

"Did you girls do that?" Mrs. Zimmer said.

"No, we told you before," Hannah said.

Emily leaned closer to the word. She smiled.

Hannah thought she would shrink back in alarm.

Even Anna was surprised. "Did you read it?"

"Do you know what *Ildred* means?" Hannah said.

Emily chuckled. "No, see there." She pointed to a letter, much smaller than the others, right against the edge of the door.

"Is that an M?" Hannah said.

For *murderer*.

"Mildred?" Anna said.

"That's my grandmother's name."

Impossible. This woman couldn't be Mildred's

granddaughter. Wait. She had the same blue eyes, the same perfect nose, and the same butter-wouldn't-melt-in-her-mouth smile.

"This must have been her room when she lived here," Emily said.

"What an interesting coincidence," Mrs. Zimmer said.

"That explains that." Emily closed the door and latched it.

"Why would she scratch her name like that? Why would she be so angry?" Hannah said.

"I don't think the writing is angry. It's messy. It can't be easy to carve your name," Emily said.

It was angry. With good reason.

Emily didn't care. The door was shut, so she checked her appearance in the mirror.

Hannah stepped between Emily and her reflection. "Did your grandmother die when she was young? Did she drown?"

"Oh, no. Mildred is very much alive." Emily smiled.

Alive? She couldn't be. After nearly eighty years?

"Then who is the girl?" Hannah said.

"What girl?" Emily said.

"The one I saw. The one with wet hair," Hannah said.

Emily smiled a different kind of smile. "Well, Hannah, as I said—"

Hannah interrupted her. "I know. Your grandmother had a sister."

A beloved sister. A girl who lived on in memory.

"No," Emily said.

No?

"Are you sure? Maybe she forgot to tell you," Hannah said.

Emily snorted in a most unattractive way. "My grandmother doesn't forget a thing."

Mildred hadn't forgotten. She was afraid. She wouldn't dare speak that name. She had to hide what she had done.

"You could ask her," Hannah said.

"I think she would have mentioned something as important as a sister."

"That's right." Mrs. Zimmer embraced her daughters and awkwardly brought them together.

Now even Hannah wasn't so sure. She glanced at the mirror and saw nothing but her own disappointed face.

So that sister was really and truly dead. No, worse than dead. If nobody knew her name, then she never even existed.

Emily walked away. As she left the room, her high heels clicked loudly against the wooden floor.

No one heard anything else. No one listened to the voices of the dead. They stood on what might as well have been the bottom of the ocean and shouted up. No one heard a girl who wasn't a girl anymore cry out with all her might, *My name is Ruth.*

"Wait," Hannah said. "Was her name Ruth?"

❧ 21 ❧

Yes. I was Ruth.

"Ruth?" Anna said. "How do you know?"

I told her.

"She told me," Hannah said.

Hannah had listened. Finally someone could. Now I had my name back. It wasn't enough for me to know it. Someone else had to distinguish me from all the other shadows.

"What do you mean, she told you?" Anna said.

"I heard her."

"I didn't hear anything."

Because you don't listen. You only care about superficial things.

Anna didn't hear that either.

Hannah ran after Emily. "Call your grandmother and ask her if her sister is named Ruth."

Emily stopped just before she reached the front door.

~126~

She watched Hannah stumble down the stairs, past the hall tree mirror. She didn't ask to borrow the telephone. She thought about how painful it was to see such a troubled child. Hannah reminded her of her own daughter—except she thought Hannah was much worse.

"Why won't you ask her?" Hannah said.

Emily sighed. Then she took Mrs. Zimmer into the living room. "It's probably none of my business. But I have a daughter. Lydia is younger than your girls. She's been seeing a therapist for three or four years now. Dr. Vivian is such a nice person. Lydia loves their chats."

"What are you trying to say?" Mrs. Zimmer said.

Emily opened her bag and found a small card in her wallet. She held it out to Mrs. Zimmer. "It's nothing to be ashamed of. We all need help coping. Especially when we live in gloomy houses."

"We're going to move as soon as our new house is ready," Mrs. Zimmer said.

"Of course you are. However, the damage may already have been done," Emily said.

"Your grandmother is the one who needs to see the doctor. She's the one who won't talk about her sister," Hannah said.

"For the last time, she doesn't have a sister," Emily snapped.

Mildred had always hated me. She wished I had never been born. She left me behind—forever. But she couldn't deny me any longer. Hannah knew. She knew.

The card quivered in Emily's hand. Didn't they see that? Didn't that show them?

Mrs. Zimmer's gaze switched back and forth between Hannah and Anna, who leaned over the banister. She thought how troubled and unhappy Hannah had been ever since they came here, how she had no idea how to help her own daughter. Then she took the card from Emily.

Hannah was shocked. Of course, my mother had also turned her back on her daughter. Hannah couldn't take comfort in that. She started to cry and ran upstairs.

"You're making the right decision. Your daughter needs serious help," Emily said.

How could she be so cruel? Had I forgotten? She was Mildred's granddaughter.

Emily opened the door and marched out of the house. She left without regret. She thought she had done a good deed. She didn't look back to see someone following her. She got into her shiny red car and turned on the engine. She was going home now. Sooner or later she would go to Mildred. And I would go with her.

Yes, I would. I was sure of it. I had my name back. I was Ruth. Ruth, Ruth, Ruth. When I met Mildred again, she wouldn't dare deny me. I would make her sorry she had tried.

The red car crept along the driveway. Emily was a cautious driver. She stopped two feet before the road. She looked right, toward the house with the cats. She looked left. Did she notice the field? Did she wonder what was beneath the yellow grass? Of course not. Mildred had never told her what happened there. Mildred had never even told her my name.

Emily waited while a black car passed like a shadow. Then she turned the wheel to the right and accelerated onto Hemlock Road. . . .

And I was left behind.

Again!

Mildred had gotten married and had children. Those children had had children. Their children had more children. And so Mildred would live on and on.

I hated her. I hated her.

If only I could tell her how much.

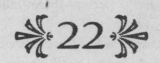

22

I paced angrily back and forth under the hemlock trees. Then I remembered I didn't have to stew all alone anymore. I could go talk with my friend. Hannah could hear me now. After nearly eighty years, there was so much I wanted to say.

I went back inside.

Mrs. Zimmer was in the dining room. She wasn't sewing; she was talking on the telephone. "I'd like to make an appointment for my daughter Hannah Zimmer. She's having issues with—" Her voice broke off for a moment.

A piece of black fabric on the table billowed up.

"She imagines she is seeing supernatural things. Only she isn't. It's just the wind."

Mrs. Zimmer slapped the cloth down. Her palm got stabbed by a pin. Ha!

"We'd like to come as soon as possible. Dr. Vivian was recommended to us by a friend."

How could Mrs. Zimmer think someone like Emily was a friend? The fabric blew over Mrs. Zimmer's face. She tore it off and threw it on the ground. She thought something not very nice even as the voice in the phone told her when and where to come. "Thank you. We'll see you next Tuesday," Mrs. Zimmer said.

Anna came into the room. "Hannah says she won't hear the voice ever again if you don't make her go."

Hannah couldn't have said that. She couldn't have. Or if she had, then she was just trying to trick Anna. She couldn't have meant it.

The bedroom door was shut. Did they think that could keep me out? Hannah was lying on Anna's bed with her head under a pillow. As if that made any difference. Little wires fed music into her ears Anna must have borrowed Selena's contraption. So what if the song was loud and cheerful. All that mattered was what was in Hannah's head.

And I knew that she was thinking, *Please go away, please don't talk to me, please leave me alone, I don't want to be crazy.*

That *was* crazy. Wasn't I the only one who listened? Wasn't I the only one who understood her? Wasn't I the only one who truly cared about her?

Hannah.

She put her hands over her ears and rocked from side to side. "No."

Just then Anna came in. "Did you say something?"

Hannah sat up and bobbed her head to the song's rhythm. "No, I didn't. I didn't hear anything. I just said 'whoa.' To the music. Whoa, whoa, whoa."

She was a terrible liar.

Even Anna knew that. She sat on the bed and hugged Hannah. She was worried about her sister. Hannah grabbed Anna and hung on for dear life. "I'm so scared," she whispered.

"It'll be okay," Anna said.

It would not be okay. These Zimmers were doing too many terrible things. Wasn't it bad enough that they planned to take away my bats? I wouldn't let them destroy my friendship.

What if Anna kept being nice to Hannah? What if she got close to Hannah again?

I needn't have worried. Anna got the red-shopping-bag book and read it out loud.

Let Anna think she was helping Hannah. Let Hannah pretend to enjoy hearing about those cruel girls. I could wait. Sooner or later night would come, as it always did, to the house on Hemlock Road.

Selena reclaimed her musical wires. Anna grew tired of reading to Hannah. Mr. and Mrs. Zimmer made one last check on Hannah. They returned to their bed, believing that Hannah slept peacefully on the top bunk.

How little they knew.

Hannah was awake. She was waiting, just as I had

waited. She knew I would never abandon her. I wouldn't let her be as alone as I had been for nearly eighty years.

Hannah?

She shook her head fiercely. She hugged her pillow. She thought, *No no no.*

I can help you.

She flipped over onto her stomach and put the pillow over her head. She thought, *Why is this happening to me?*

Because you're the only one who cares.

"I don't care anymore," she whispered.

She was lying. She had to be. I couldn't bear it if she was telling the truth.

You can prove there was a Ruth.

"No one believes me."

I can show you something. Don't you want to see?

"What is it?"

Anna turned in her sleep and heard Hannah.

Shhh.

Hannah should realize she didn't need to talk. She couldn't have any secrets from me. Nothing could come between us—not even Anna.

"You okay?" Anna peeked over the edge of her sister's mattress.

"Mmmm?" Hannah said, as if she had been sleeping.

"You want to come in bed with me?" Anna said.

No.

"Why not?" Anna said.

Had she heard me?

"Too tired," Hannah said.

Anna lowered herself back onto her bed.

Hannah and I waited—and waited—until Anna fell back asleep.

When it was quiet enough so that even the most nervous mouse found the courage to sniff at Anna's shoe, I told Hannah what to do.

Come to the attic.

Humans were so noisy. Hannah hadn't been up and down those steps often enough to know the third one had the squeak and the sixth had the bent nail, which could hurt a bare foot.

By the time we got to the top, the bats had gone hunting for the night. That was a good thing. I didn't want Hannah to be scared of them. They only had two days left. She could still save them—after I helped Hannah.

"Now what?" she whispered.

It was hard for her to get out of the habit of talking. *Come ahead.*

She tentatively felt her way through the darkness. She was frightened and worried she would bump into a bat. I kept saying, *Step, step, step.* So she did.

I wasn't quite sure where I had hidden it. It had been almost eighty years. Besides, I had been in such a rush that day. I had heard them downstairs taking my books from the shelves in my room. I had heard my father shouting, *Where is that Ruth?* I had felt so smart to remember what I had left in the attic that very morning. Yes, I always thought I knew so much. I had even seen Mildred allow poor Whiskers to be murdered. So why hadn't I known what else she would do?

"Are you angry?" Hannah said.

No.

"Yes, you are." Hannah was afraid.

Not anymore. Instead I thought about which board.

It's there. Reach under.

She knelt down and stuck her arm in the gap where the floor crossed the eaves. She pulled out a fluffy mess.

Those mice, those dim-witted mice. What had they done?

"It's a book."

It used to be. It wasn't anymore. It was a horrible mess.

She brushed off the fluff. "It doesn't have a cover or a title page."

Half the first page was gone. So the best book in the whole world began—

> We are the Bastables. There are six of us
> besides Father. Our mother is dead, and if
> you think we don't care because I don't
> tell you much about her, you only show that
> you do not understand people at all.

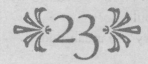

We couldn't read much that night. The attic was too dark and smelly for Hannah to stay up there long. The very next day, Hannah said she wasn't able to go to school. Mrs. Zimmer didn't argue. So Hannah lay on her bed. We read the entire book all in one gulp. The Bastable children were exactly the same after nearly eighty years. They hadn't died. They hadn't even aged. Their adventures were still funny and scary and sad. And the children still found their treasure and lived happily ever after in the end. That is the magic of books.

I had the best day ever. Hannah loved their story too. She told me that she knew E. Nesbit because she had read something called *Five Children and It,* which didn't sound nearly so nice but Hannah said it was good too.

No one could be as happy as I was, not even the

Bastable children after they made friends with the uncle from India.

The only bad part was when Mrs. Zimmer came upstairs to see what Hannah wanted for lunch. "What are you reading?" she asked.

"Oh, just a book I found." Hannah said.

That was her chance to say, *A book that Ruth hid in the attic nearly eighty years ago when she was alive.*

Only Hannah didn't. Hannah, in fact, was deliberately not saying it. As she was going to bed, she told her parents she hadn't heard any voices all day and so she didn't have to go see Dr. Vivian because she was cured.

Didn't she understand? They wouldn't think she was crazy if she proved that I was there.

At seven o'clock in the morning, Mrs. Zimmer made Hannah get up and get dressed.

"I think school will still be too upsetting for me," Hannah said.

"The pest-control people are coming. That will be even more upsetting," Mrs. Zimmer said.

The day had come.

Hannah had to stay home. Together we could outwit the enemy. We could be as brave as Oswald when he battled the burglar. We could save the bats.

Save the bats.

"Don't let those people hurt the bats. Please, Mom. We're going to be moving soon anyway. Why can't we leave the bats alone?" Hannah said.

"No one is going to hurt them. I'm sure the pest-control people have a safe way to persuade them to leave," Mrs. Zimmer said.

How?

"How?" Hannah said.

"I don't know. I just know that there are laws to protect bats."

What good was that? There are laws against murder too.

"Hurry up and get dressed. And *please* don't wear that T-shirt again."

Hannah disobeyed her mother by putting on the Park Slope shirt, but she had to go to school.

I couldn't be mad at her. She tried. She also left my book lying open on her bed so I could move the pages.

How could I read? The day would be too terrible.

The parents thought that too. Mrs. Zimmer drove off. Mr. Zimmer had to stay home to deal with the pest-control people. He escaped into his music. He turned it up so loud the windows vibrated. He danced around and pretended to play instruments until someone knocked on the front door.

Two men stood on the porch. One was tall; the other was wide. If nothing bad was going to happen, why were they wearing masks around their necks and thick gloves?

Mr. Zimmer led them to the attic. Heavy boots clomped on the stairs.

"Are you going to trap them?" Mr. Zimmer said.

"We don't need to," the tall man said.

"You mean you just . . ." Mr. Zimmer didn't know how to say the word *kill*, even though he was perfectly capable of paying these men to do it.

The wide man laughed. "Can't anymore."

"We plug all the holes around your attic—except one. We put a one-way door in that. The bats go out to hunt just like always," the tall man said.

"Except they can't get back in."

Both men laughed.

Where would the bats go? Where would they sleep? Where would they belong?

When the men reached the attic, they slid the masks over their mouths and noses. The bats stirred uneasily in their sleep as the men tramped around.

"Wow," the tall man said.

"Must be nearly a hundred of them," the wide man said.

"Look at all that guano."

"These bats have been here for years."

Yes, nearly eighty years ago, the first bat had come.

I had been in the attic. I had nowhere else to go. I was trying to get my book. The dark shadow scared me. I didn't know what it was. Or what world I was in. More bats came. Only I didn't want them. I wanted my family.

I hated the bats until they had their babies. Then there was something I could love in the house. Something with life.

The tall man waved his arm and startled a few bats. They flew outside into the glare of unfamiliar light.

"Let's get it done," the wide man said.

No!

A wind blew a cloud of brown dust in their faces. All they thought was that they were glad to be wearing those masks.

The men tramped downstairs.

Mr. Zimmer's music got louder. Drums banged, instruments screeched, and women's voices wailed.

The bats wrapped their wings around their furry bodies and went back to sleep.

The attic was dark except for a faint ring of gold around the edges. A hint of sunlight marked the places where the bats could come and go and return again.

SLAP. A piece of wood blocked the crack by the corner and shut out the light. Could a wind blow away the wood? No. *BAP BAP BAP BAP BAP.* A gun spat sharp bits of metal into it.

BAP BAP BAP BAP BAP. The whole house shook from the attack. The mice fled in terror. The spiders abandoned their webs.

BAP BAP BAP BAP BAP.

It was too much to bear. But I couldn't leave the attic. I had to stay with my beautiful bats.

BAP BAP BAP BAP BAP.

They huddled in the rafters. Mothers spread their wings around their babies.

BAP BAP BAP BAP BAP.

Bit by bit, the darkness grew. Piece by piece, those men took away the light.

And then it was finished. The attic was black except for that one small place where the bats would leave and never ever return.

Where was Hannah? If she came home, she could plug the hole. Then the bats couldn't leave.

Where was Hannah?

Those men were downstairs. Mr. Zimmer paid them.

"It'll cost you another five hundred to clean up that guano," the tall man said.

"You got a lot up there," the wide man said.

Mr. Zimmer shook his head. "We're just renting. We won't be here that much longer."

Of course. The Zimmers would leave too. They would put Hannah in the car and take her away from me.

Then there would be nothing.

I went back to the attic. The bats still clung to the rafters. If only there was some way to plug the hole. If they didn't leave, they could stay with me in the attic.

If they didn't go out to hunt, eventually the bats would die.

24

Where was Hannah? Why didn't she come home?

Selena did. She squealed with delight when her father told her the news. Then she called Marcus to tell him. It was easy to hear her voice through the attic floor.

"I was thinking you could come over tomorrow night. To study." She laughed.

It wasn't fair that she should be so happy. She should suffer for what she had done. If only she could.

"See you tomorrow," she said.

No one would see the bats tomorrow. They were waking up now. They unfurled their wings and stretched. Then they let go of the rafters. The great gray beast swirled through the empty space. Could it really be their last dance with me?

The bats tried to leave. They were confused that most

of the holes were gone. They were hungry. They had to find a way outside so they could eat.

No!

Where was Hannah? Why wasn't she here to stop them?

One by one, the bats squeezed through the small hole.

Wait!

Did they all have to leave me?

Yes.

They weren't as cruel as the family who drove away nearly eighty years ago. The bats didn't know they wouldn't be able to return. They didn't know that a selfish teenage girl had robbed them of their home.

She had driven away the good. Now only the filth remained.

A breeze began to blow toward the northeast corner of the attic. Toward the place above Selena's room. Anger always made that breeze stronger.

There was a pile of bat dirt above Selena's bed by the time the car stopped in the driveway. The front door opened. Anna's voice called out, "We're home."

The wind didn't stop blowing.

The voices from downstairs sounded far away.

"The bats are gone. Isn't that wonderful?" Selena said.

Wasn't it wonderful how the filth piled up on the attic floor?

"Where have you been?" Mr. Zimmer said.

"I took the girls to look at the new house," Mrs. Zimmer said.

"Mom picked us up so Hannah wouldn't have to ride the bus," Anna said.

"Why?" Mr. Zimmer said.

"She was worried that Georgia might tease me. But Georgia has nothing to tease me about because I'm not crazy," Hannah said.

"Nothing unusual happened to you today?" Mr. Zimmer said.

"No." Hannah spoke firmly.

She was pretending. I knew that. I knew that was why she laughed and talked so loudly with her parents.

After their dinner, she could have found me. She knew I had had a horrible day. A friend would say how sorry she was—even if that wouldn't bring back the bats.

Hannah didn't come looking for me. And I couldn't go to her. I had a lot to do in the attic before Marcus came on Saturday night.

Shortly before dawn, the bats tried to come back. I hated hearing their cries of confusion as they bumped against the house.

The wind swirled across the attic floor. The mountain of filth got bigger. Still it wasn't quite heavy enough—yet.

Just when the bats would have begun their nightly dance, the doorbell rang.

No one answered at first.

The doorbell rang again. Marcus was impatient. I was too.

Then the front door opened and Selena said, "Hi."

"Hi," Marcus said.

Their voices echoed through the silent house.

"Come on up to my room."

The steps creaked as they climbed. She giggled. They thought they had privacy. Their voices were easily heard through the attic floor.

"Nice room," he said.

"Shall we study?" she said.

"I am. I'm studying you," he said.

He thought he was so funny.

A creaking sound as first one person and then another sank onto the bed.

"Study hard. I'm going to give you a test," she said.

"I bet I get an A-plus," he said.

The bed creaked again.

"What's that splotch on your ceiling?" He sounded worried.

"That's always been there," she said.

Had it?

"Dad won't paint it. He never does anything *I* want him to," she said.

"He did get rid of the bats, didn't he?" he said.

Yes, Mr. Zimmer did. Because Selena asked him to.

They were silent. They must have been kissing. Like Mildred and her beau, so busy with each other, they couldn't care about whether anybody else lived or died.

The wind in the attic blew harder. It got its fingers in the cracks between the floorboards. It found the holes.

There was always a weak spot. A place that couldn't stand any more. It had been pushed too hard for too long. Where was that spot?

The wind whistled across the floor.

"Ruth."

Hannah's head appeared at the entrance to the attic. She had come to see her friend after all. Only she wasn't thinking sympathetic thoughts. She was worried.

"I heard a noise. What's going on up here? What are you doing?"

Had she forgotten about the bats? I hadn't. Maybe others could ignore a crime. But I would make sure the guilty people got punished.

The cloud of dust made Hannah cough. "Stop it, Ruth."

Stop it, Ruth. That was what Mildred always said. No matter what I did. Dancing around to show her a book. Begging her to fix my hair. Asking her to hunt for treasure like the Bastable children so we could restore our family's fortune. No matter what I wanted, she always said, *Stop it, Ruth.*

"Stop it, Ruth."

Hannah shouldn't have said that to me. Why should I stop? No one else did. Everybody did whatever they wanted to spoil the things I loved.

So I didn't stop.

Hannah came toward the dust cloud. Her feet shook the floorboards. The ceiling plaster cracked.

Now there was a small hole. I could see some dust drift down on the lovebirds.

His nose wrinkled. He smelled something foul. She smelled it too. She thought it was his socks. They stopped kissing.

He looked up at the ceiling. A lovely fear filled his eyes when he saw a chunk of plaster swing loose. He jumped up just as the huge mountain of guano buried Selena on her bed.

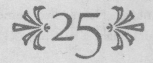

When disaster struck, you found out who really loved you. When you were covered with bat droppings, or tangled with weeds underwater, would someone come to your rescue? Would someone hold out his hand to pull you up from death? Or would he step farther away and brush the brown filth off his black shirt?

Selena hadn't moved. Was she dead?

No. She was waiting to be saved. She raised one hand, pleading for help from her beloved. Her palm was covered with a small heap of dark brown droppings.

"What happened?" Marcus said.

Selena didn't know. Besides, she couldn't scream or even speak without getting bat dirt in her mouth.

Mr. and Mrs. Zimmer rushed up the stairs and knocked on the door. "Selena?"

They came in, with cries of amazement and concern. Anna quickly followed her parents. She stared through the gaping hole in the ceiling. What did she think she would see?

Mrs. Zimmer hurried over to help Selena stand. As Selena struggled to rise from the chunks of ceiling and mounds of bat droppings, she resembled a rotting corpse rising from the grave.

This was too much for Marcus. He took a step toward the door.

"You're not going, are you?" Selena spluttered through the brown.

Marcus shook his head no, then nodded yes. He ran from the room so fast that he tripped and stumbled all the way down the stairs. His car's engine roared loudly to life. The Zimmers all listened to the sound fade as it traveled along Hemlock Road. This time that boy would be gone for good. Ha!

Selena buried her face in the towel Mrs. Zimmer gave her and sobbed.

Mr. Zimmer walked around the rubble.

Anna wrinkled her nose. "That's what we smelled in the closet. You see, there *is* an explanation. Hannah?"

Hannah wasn't there.

"The men said we needed to get that guano cleaned up," Mr. Zimmer said.

"Why didn't you? Now Marcus will never come back. He'll never even speak to me again after seeing me like this!" Selena cried.

"He can't blame you. It's not *your* fault," Mrs. Zimmer said.

Yes, it was.

Hannah came in. She didn't accuse Selena. She said, "Are you all right?"

"No!" Selena wailed.

"You'll feel better after you have a shower. Girls, get some clean clothes for your sister," Mrs. Zimmer said.

Hannah went to the dresser and got a shirt. Why was she helping Selena? She should want her to be miserable.

"You need clean clothes too. What's on your shirt?" Mrs. Zimmer said.

Everyone stared at Hannah.

"*You* were in the attic," Selena said.

Hannah couldn't deny it. Bits of guano fell from her hair.

"What were you doing up there?" Anna said.

"You wanted to play another trick. You made the ceiling collapse," Selena said.

"Oh no," Mrs. Zimmer said.

"It was an accident," Hannah said.

"Didn't we make ourselves clear?" Mr. Zimmer said.

"I tried to be so nice to you because you're having a breakdown and everything and look what you do. You ruined my entire life," Selena said.

At least Selena still had a life. She didn't think of that. Or what she had done. She just stood there, shouting at poor Hannah.

Who wasn't defending herself. I had to do something.

I went back up in the attic and blew a nice fresh pile of dirt down on all that golden hair.

"Stop it, Ruth!" Hannah shouted.

She realized what she had said. She clapped her hands over her mouth. It was too late. She couldn't pretend I wasn't there anymore.

"Oh no." Anna was disappointed.

"I suppose you think if you act crazy no one will punish you. You're wrong. You're in so much trouble. Isn't she, Dad?" Selena said.

Mr. Zimmer looked at Mrs. Zimmer. He didn't know what to think. He raised his hands. Then he let them fall. "I better get a broom and clean this up."

"You have to punish her," Selena said.

"Hannah," Mrs. Zimmer said.

Hannah looked at her mother like she was going to cry.

Then Mrs. Zimmer said, "Go to your room."

Hannah ran before her tears could fall.

"That's it? That's all you're going to do? Look at this mess. Where will I sleep? What will I wear?"

Hannah didn't go to her room. She knew Anna would follow her there. She went outside and sat next to the house, under the chokeberry bush.

Of course I went too.

I blew on her cheek.

She turned her face away. "You shouldn't have done that to Selena." She was thinking I shouldn't have done it to *her*.

Only I hadn't done anything to her. I wouldn't. She was my friend. I was the only one who really cared about her. I was the only one who understood her.

A few bats swooped past the hemlock trees. Hannah pointed to them. "You see? The bats weren't killed. They survived."

They can't go home.

"They'll find a place to live nearby and you can still see them."

They won't be with me. Didn't she understand?

Actually she did.

"I'm sorry. When we leave, I'll make holes so they can come back in the attic. Would you like that?"

No. I would *not* like it when the family left. But being with Hannah, and watching the bats circle in front of the moon, made me feel peaceful and hopeful. Maybe Hannah wouldn't leave. Maybe something would happen. Maybe I could think of what to do to keep her from leaving me. Maybe I wouldn't have to be alone again.

The front door banged. Anna came outside to ruin everything. "You were supposed to go to our room. You better go before Selena finds you."

"She won't find me unless you *tell*," Hannah said.

Anna sat down next to Hannah. Right where I had been.

"I would never do that." Anna thought how she didn't want to make things worse. She broke a branch off the bush and snapped it into smaller bits.

"So, are you still hearing things?" Anna said.

"I don't hear *things*, I hear Ruth," Hannah said.

Anna sighed.

"I know what she's thinking. She hates Selena. I think because Selena reminds her of her sister Mildred. I haven't figured out what the soldier has to do with it. I just know something terrible happened to Ruth and she's very unhappy."

"You're unhappy." Anna thought that was why Hannah thought these things.

"That has nothing to do with it. Ruth is real. She'll prove it to you. She'll make the branch wave. Ruth, show Anna."

I started to, of course. If your friend asks you to do something, you do it.

Then I stopped.

"Come on, Ruth. I know you're still here. Why won't you show Anna?"

Hannah's voice was desperate. I held completely still. I didn't want to reveal myself to Anna. I didn't want Anna as a friend. I only wanted Hannah.

❦·26·❦

"She's playing a trick. She likes to do that. Don't you, Ruth?" Hannah was getting frantic.

Anna pitied Hannah so much she patted her sister's knee.

Hannah pushed her hand away and shouted, "Show her, Ruth!"

Selena's face appeared in the living room window. "Mom! Hannah didn't go to her room. She's outside with Anna. I heard her. She isn't sorry one bit. You have to make her suffer like I'm suffering."

That was what Mildred said—right before they took away all my books.

"Hannah Zimmer, you are in big trouble now," Mrs. Zimmer said.

Two sets of angry feet stomped down the stairs and

out onto the porch. Mother and father stood right by the chokeberry bush. Would Hannah have to cut a switch?

"Tomorrow you will clean up Selena's room. Tonight Selena will sleep in your bed and you'll sleep on the sofa. Now go get your pajamas on," Mrs. Zimmer said.

"It isn't nine o'clock." Hannah thought how humiliating it was to be punished.

"You're going to bed right this minute. And there will be *no* reading," Mrs. Zimmer said.

"Not even a little?" Hannah badly needed the comfort of a book that night.

"You heard your mother. Now march," Mr. Zimmer said.

Hannah dragged her feet up the stairs.

Selena said, "Mom, she isn't marching."

"Hurry up, Hannah. Stop daydreaming. It's no wonder . . ."

Mrs. Zimmer didn't have to finish the sentence. Hannah knew her mother thought Hannah had lost her mind. She started to wonder how she could tell if she had.

Oh, everyone was feeling worse and worse—including me. How could they treat Hannah this way? Obviously her family didn't care about her at all. Not like I did.

Upstairs the yelling continued. "Brush your teeth. Put on that nightgown. Don't even *look* at that book."

Finally an exhausted Hannah lay down on the sofa. Of course she couldn't sleep. Not when Selena and Anna were whispering about her upstairs in her room.

"Do you think Hannah really believes she hears things?" Selena asked.

"I don't know," Anna said.

"I think she's just trying to get attention," Selena said.

"When we were outside, she said Ruth would make the branch of that red bush wave," Anna remembered.

"That is crazy," Selena said.

"I know," Anna agreed.

"She used to be so smart," Selena said.

Hannah whimpered a little as she wondered whether Selena was right.

You are smart, I told her. I wanted to make her feel better. *You're smart and good and a wonderful friend.*

Only we both knew that what I thought hardly mattered. Not while her family was there to make her so miserable.

I wished there was some way to get her away from them. Unfortunately the opposite was going to happen. Sooner or later they would take Hannah away from me. Sooner or later Hannah would drive off with the ones who hated her. And I would be left alone again.

I didn't think I could bear that. I would do anything to keep that from happening.

And then I had an idea of how I could keep Hannah with me.

Ruth? What's going on?

It was such a strong idea that I couldn't think about it near her. I left the room.

I went outside. Bats circled the hemlock trees, darting

back and forth across the property line. I tried to go with them. Just to see.

I couldn't, of course. Only maybe it wouldn't matter that I couldn't leave. Maybe soon.

If I could.

If Hannah would agree.

Or if Hannah wouldn't know.

Was it right? Or was it wrong? Did it matter? It was the only way.

The house on Hemlock Road was dark except for a light in Selena's room. What was going on in there?

The parents were cleaning up. They had changed their minds about making Hannah do it. Mrs. Zimmer put clothes in a big plastic bag. Mr. Zimmer's broom swished across the floor. It wasn't a comforting sound. He had tied a scarf over his mouth. He looked like a thief. In fact, he had decided to steal something from me—my friend.

"We can't stay in the house another night." He banged the broom against the floor. A cloud of dust swirled around his head. He didn't realize it was a larger cloud than it should have been.

"We can't live in the new house. There's no plumbing," she said.

"We'll go to a motel."

"Can we afford it?"

"Can we afford not to? We have to get Hannah away from here before she really goes crazy."

"Are you blaming the house?"

"Of course not. I don't know. Maybe we haven't been

firm enough with her. Or with any of them. The point is we can't stay here."

"Okay. We'll leave tomorrow."

Tomorrow? That was so soon. There was no time to consider. I would have only one chance to save Hannah—and myself.

❊·27·❊

The moon began to sink behind the house on Hemlock Road.

In just a few hours, the sun would rise. The day would come. And Hannah would go. Unless . . .

Was it time?

The dust had settled in Selena's room. The hole in the ceiling seemed like an entryway to another world. It wasn't.

A mouse peeped around the edge of the door and then ran away.

The mice would miss the Zimmers—after the food was gone.

Tiny red lights blinked in the biggest bedroom. Would Mr. and Mrs. Zimmer think that was a warning? Oh no. They would have been comforted to know their electric contraptions were still working. That didn't keep them awake. They dreamed their dreams, buried by blankets. Mr. Zimmer battled a brown tornado with a broom. Mrs. Zimmer made the twins adorable outfits. In her dream, the girls were identical.

Didn't she know that Hannah was nothing like Anna?

Someone had pulled Hannah's mattress on the floor. Naturally Selena wouldn't have wanted to sleep so close to the attic. Her golden hair was spread across her pillow. Her lips were slightly parted. She breathed the name *Marcus*. She was a tempting target.

So was Anna, who clutched the red-shopping-bag book as if it were a life preserver. It wouldn't save her. She would be sorry. Oh yes. For now, she slept. She dreamed she had to visit Hannah in a hospital.

I knew that would never happen.

Down the steps, past the hall tree mirror, into the living room, where Hannah tossed and turned on the sofa.

Her sleep wasn't deep enough for dreams.

I blew gently on her cheek. She thought it was a bug to brush away. I blew again. Now she was awake. She pulled the blanket over her head and uncovered her feet.

Do you want to know what happened to me?

Her eyes popped open. *Yes.*

She was thinking that if she found out, then she could help me be happy.

She would make me happy. She just didn't know how—yet.

It was all Mildred's fault.

Hannah nodded. She knew what older sisters could do.

She had an orange fluffy cat. It didn't like me. It never let me hold it. Mildred said I didn't know how. I got my own pet—a mouse with a bent leg. I named him Whiskers. He let me stroke his fur. One day the cat chased him into Mildred's closet. And killed him.

Mildred didn't save him?

I knew Hannah would understand.

Then what happened, Ruth?

I went in the closet. I carved Mildred's name on the door so everyone would know she let Whiskers die. I wanted her to suffer, so I cut up all her dresses.

Did you get in trouble?

They took all my books except The Story of the Treasure Seekers. *I had hidden it in the attic.*

So what happened to you?

That was harder to say.

I'll show you.

How?

Come outside with me.

Now?

Now.

The blanket slipped from around her shoulders as she tiptoed to the door. She turned the knob.

Let the door not squeak.

Let the night be still.

She danced across the grass. The dew must have felt cold on her bare feet. She shivered. She hurried toward the road.

Not that way. Mildred went across the driveway, with her beau. So I snuck around the back.

Hannah came with me past the chokeberry bush and past the ash tree where the cat had climbed.

Let the cats be quiet. Let them stalk in silence. Let them hunt their own prey.

Let Hannah find the way to be with me. Forever.

Where were you going? Hannah thought.

To spy on the lovebirds.

Why?

So I could tell my father what they did. Then he would punish her.

We passed the garden of weeds. When we reached the top of the ditch, we stopped. The moon seemed to be sinking into the golden grass.

I saw them over there, not far from the road, on the opposite side of the pond.

What pond? Hannah was puzzled.

The field was a pond then.

Before.

Let her not ask why.

Mildred and her beau were sitting together on the ground.

Did you hide by those rocks?

Hannah ran down into the ditch, where I couldn't go. She crossed the path, where Lieutenant Maplethorpe paced back and forth defending his property. Back and forth, day after day, still fighting his war.

I couldn't hide. Mildred saw me. She pointed and said, "Look out! The enemy approaches!"

Hannah ran up the other side of the ditch.

It was about to happen. She wasn't far from the great gray rocks where the soldier had hidden himself. She ran toward the place.

Her nightgown was so white in the moonlight. She seemed to float above the ground. Like she was already a ghost.

Like she was the girl behind the glass.

Then she would be stuck—with me. She couldn't leave, couldn't live, could never be loved.

I knew full well how horribly she would suffer.

What was I doing? I loved Hannah. It was wrong to want her to be with me. It was selfish.

I had to stop her. But how? I couldn't cross the ditch.

Hannah was close to the yellow field. When she got there, she would fall in because it wasn't grass. It was a foul black swamp.

And when she tried to scream, water would fill her open mouth, just as it had done to mine all those years ago.

She reached the edge.

Hannah, wait!

She didn't stop. She walked into the grass. Why wasn't she listening to me?

Someone had to help her. Someone had to save her. Someone had to hear me.

But who?

28

I had to get help, even though that meant leaving Hannah.

I hurried back to the house. Anna was still asleep in her bed. Only now she dreamed that she wandered the halls of the hospital, looking for Hannah.

Wake up, wake up.

I blew on Anna's face.

She groaned and rolled over.

Save her!

She opened one eye.

You have to hear me now. You have to.

She wouldn't listen. She never had before.

Get up. Look out the window. Save Hannah.

Anna thought this was another dream—a bad one. I had to make her understand.

If you don't, Hannah will become Ruth.

Anna sat up. She jumped out of bed and stepped over Selena.

She's sinking in the muck.

Anna ran to the window. She saw a white shape in the dark field. She saw one arm wave and then disappear.

I was too late. Anna had been too stubborn. Now she was too slow.

Anna screamed, "Wake up, wake up! Hannah's in trouble!"

She ran down the stairs, out the door, and across the yard.

I didn't wait to watch the parents get up. I rushed back to the edge.

Hannah was sinking. The muck blackened the nightgown. It pulled her down and down through the earth. The dark would get darker than any night she had ever known. She was so scared. Just like I had been when I had clutched at the water. I had nothing to hold on to. So I felt life slip from my grasp.

Anna ran down the ditch and up the other side. She stopped at the part that was still solid ground. She reached toward her sister. Hannah's arms flailed. Black drops splattered across Anna's face.

Anna's arms were too short. She leaned closer. She got hold of Hannah's hand. Then Anna slipped. She was sinking too. Hannah was dragging her down.

Somehow Anna scrambled back to solid ground. She pulled Hannah out of the muck.

The sisters lay side by side on the ground. Anna's chest heaved as she struggled to get her breath back. But Hannah was frighteningly still.

Mr. Zimmer came running. He stuck his fingers into Hannah's mouth. He cleared out a glob of muck. He bent over and breathed into her. He thought how he would give her his life if he could. He breathed and breathed again and again. Finally Hannah coughed and spluttered.

Mrs. Zimmer and Selena came. "The ambulance is on its way," Mrs. Zimmer said.

Mr. Zimmer picked Hannah up in his arms. Mrs. Zimmer brushed the hair back from Hannah's face. Selena hugged Anna. They all walked to the front of the house. The siren got closer and closer.

"How did you know she was out there?" Mrs. Zimmer asked Anna.

"I just knew because . . ." Anna paused.

Would she say it? Would she admit it?

"Ruth told me," Anna said.

Mrs. Zimmer hugged Anna tight. She thought she must keep her other daughter from slipping into madness. She said, "We're leaving this house tonight."

The ambulance arrived. The men put Hannah on a cot and wheeled it into the back. Mrs. Zimmer got in with her. The doors slammed shut. The red light whirled and the siren wailed as the ambulance took away my Hannah.

Mr. Zimmer packed a few things in a little suitcase. Then he and the girls got in the car. "You saved your sister," Mr. Zimmer said to Anna.

"I already told you it was Ruth," Anna said.

He shook his head and started the engine.

I howled as the car drove off toward the pink sky that was just barely visible beyond the hemlock trees.

Yes, I had saved Hannah. But no one had saved me.

Saving Hannah was the right thing to do.

But it didn't make me happy.

The worst part was not knowing if she was really all right.

After all, an ambulance had taken Miz D to the hospital and she had died.

I thought I would know if Hannah had crossed over. Then I realized. She would have gone to some other, better world. Where I would never be allowed to go because I still couldn't leave this place on Hemlock Road.

Now that I had selfishly wanted to keep Hannah, I didn't think I ever would.

Days passed. The nights got darker because the moon got smaller.

Why didn't the Zimmers come back? Were they just

going to leave their belongings? Even if Selena wouldn't want her filthy clothes, what about the others?

The mice were thrilled. They gorged on the food. The spiders constructed elaborate webs across doorways where no one ever walked.

And what did I do? What could I do? My precious book was stuck behind the bunk beds. I couldn't even console myself with the Bastable children. I clung to my memory of the day Hannah and I had read it together. I tried to keep anger from rising up and ruining everything.

Oh, it was terrible. I waited by the front door. I watched for the family to return. Each car that passed took away a part of me.

Hoping hurt.

Then one morning the silver car turned into the driveway. I didn't know what day it was. I had lost track. It didn't matter. Who was in the car? It was hard to see. Mr. Zimmer drove. Mrs. Zimmer sat next to him. Selena was in the back. Next to her was Anna. Where was Hannah?

"Let's get this over with," Mr. Zimmer said.

All four jumped out of the car. They were thinking of what to pack now, what could come later.

Then Hannah got out.

Hannah! Are you all right?

She nodded. She was trying not to think bad thoughts, but the house horrified her.

I followed her inside. I had so much to tell her. So much I wanted to find out. I rambled on about mice and spiders until she found the book behind the bed. She held it out in front of her. *Where should I put it? Would it be easier to read if I took the pages apart?*

Then I understood. She wanted to do something kind for me before she left—forever.

No!

I didn't want this. I couldn't bear this. I wasn't brave enough to say good-bye.

I went outside. I didn't want to watch the packing. I could hear their voices as I paced back and forth under the hemlock trees.

Mr. Zimmer said, "Hurry."

Mrs. Zimmer said, "I can't find my scissors."

Selena said, "I'll have to get a whole new wardrobe."

Anna said, "Should I help you pack, Hannah?"

Hannah said nothing at all.

Another car stopped behind the Zimmers' car. It was red. That should have been a warning.

Emily got out. "I hope whatever you have to do here won't take long. Saturdays are very busy for us. Lydia has flute at twelve, French at one-thirty, and her therapist at three."

A girl slumped in the backseat on the driver's side, chewing viciously on her thumbnail. The door on the right rear side opened. A cane waved in the air. Emily came around and pulled someone's arm.

A very old woman stood hunched over a cane, teetering on the uneven ground. She tilted her head to stare at the house on Hemlock Road.

"Here it is. After nearly eighty years," she said.

It was Mildred.

Mildred's soft pretty skin sagged in wrinkles. Her long blond hair was twisted into a small white bun. Her fingers were bent like claws. Her back was humped. Her blue eyes blinked behind thick glasses. She was a very old person. Why, she must have been nearly ninety-five.

I wasn't.

I could never grow older.

Mildred hobbled across the driveway, around the house.

"Where are you going, Grandmother?" Emily said.

"To the pond." Mildred's words caught in her throat. She hurried a little, as if she were still trying to keep me from following her. She stopped when she reached the backyard. "Where is it?" She shook her cane at Emily. "What happened to the pond?"

Mildred knew perfectly well what had happened.

Even if she hadn't been there, she must have heard how the Maplethorpes filled it in, how they moved their son away so they could pretend like nothing had ever happened, like no one had ever died.

"You told me that little girl nearly drowned here," Mildred said.

"It's a swamp. You can drown in a swamp. Anyway, she didn't," Emily said.

Someone else did. Would Mildred admit that? It was hard to tell what that old brain thought. She wobbled, until Emily grabbed hold of her to steady her.

"Are you all right?" Emily said.

Mildred shook her head. Tears flooded her face.

Emily found a handkerchief in her purse and blotted Mildred's withered cheeks. "Now, now, Grandmother."

She didn't weep like the young Mildred would have, daintily dabbing at her eyes. This old Mildred sobbed.

"What's the matter with her?" Lydia said.

Emily awkwardly patted Mildred's shoulder. "She gets this way. The staff at the care center don't know why."

"Because I'm dying," Mildred spluttered. "I'm dying, and I'm scared."

She was scared to meet me. As well she should be.

"You aren't dying today," Lydia said.

"I thought about it. I thought if I went in the pond, that would put an end to it," Mildred said.

"Oh, Grandmother, what a thing to say. Is that why you wanted me to bring you here? We're leaving right now." Emily was shocked.

"An end to what?" Lydia said.

Mildred didn't answer. She couldn't admit what she had done.

The wind blew. A leaf tore loose and whirled past Mildred's face. Of course she ignored it. She let Emily lead her back.

Mrs. Zimmer came out of the house. "I thought I recognized the car."

Emily introduced everybody to each other—except of course me.

"I'd invite you in, but we're just here to pick up a few things," Mrs. Zimmer said.

"I'm glad to see you took my advice. We're leaving too. Come on, Lydia, help your great-grandmother," Emily said.

Lydia took Mildred's arm and walked toward the car.

Hannah and Anna came out of the house. Hannah was holding my book. She carried it over to Mildred. As she walked, loose pages fluttered to the ground.

"What's this? I can't see. What book is it?" Mildred said.

"The Bastable children. *The Story of the Treasure Seekers,*" Hannah said.

Mildred covered her mouth with her hand. She thought, *Ruthie.* She said nothing. She touched the book with a bent finger. "Where did you find it?"

"In the attic under the floorboards. Ruth told me where it was," Hannah said.

Emily turned to Mildred. She expected that Mildred would put a stop to this. But Mildred had turned white and dropped her cane.

"How did you know her name?" Mildred said.

"She told me," Hannah said.

Emily picked up the cane and took Mildred's arm. "My grandmother is a very old lady. Please don't upset her any more."

Mildred shook off Emily's hand. "The girl is right. My sister's name is Ruth."

Emily's mouth dropped open. Ha! Too bad she didn't swallow a bug. "How could I know? You never said."

"Nobody talks to each other in this family because nobody listens," Mildred said.

Then an amazing thing happened. Emily did listen. In fact, everybody stood there for a whole minute trying to hear me.

"Is she talking to you now?" Mildred said.

Yes.

Hannah nodded.

"I can't hear anything," Lydia said.

"Can you hear her too?" Mildred said to Anna.

"Not as well as Hannah. But I have heard her. That's how I knew Hannah was drowning in the swamp," Anna said.

Mildred pressed her lips into a line. She stroked the chewed edge of the book. "Did Ruthie tell you about the . . . accident?"

Accident? Oops, I dropped the gravy boat. Oops, I spilled the milk. Oops, I tore the page in your movie magazine.

A wind blew up Mildred's skirt. Her underwear was shocking and she knew it. She frantically beat at her skirt, trying to make it go down.

"Stop it, Ruth!" Mildred shook her fist at the sky. "You always were a pesky brat. Being dead hasn't made you into a better person."

You're still selfish and vain and cruel.

"Cruel?" Hannah said.

"Is she talking to you?" Mildred said.

Hannah nodded.

"Talk to me. Why won't she talk to me?" Lydia said.

So I did. I went right to her and said, *Shush.*

Her eyes got wide and she put her hand over her ear. And she shushed.

"What happened to Ruth?" Hannah said.

"Did she drown?" Anna said.

"Over there?" Hannah pointed to the yellow grass.

Mildred nodded. Tears rimmed her eyes. "It really was an accident, Ruthie."

It wasn't an accident. It was Mildred's fault. Did she hear that? No. She never listened to me—alive or dead.

"Then what about Lieutenant Maplethorpe?" Hannah said.

"You know about him too?" Mildred said.

"Not much," Hannah said.

"His family lived on the far side of the pond in a splendid house. After the war, the lieutenant wasn't quite right. Years later, he thought he was still on the front lines. He kept defending his property."

Pacing back and forth and back and forth.

"Mother and Father always told us just to leave him alone. Do not go on his land. Do not go near the pond. Do not go past the ditch."

Everybody turned to look at it. Mildred plucked at her skirt.

"I've never talked about this. We weren't supposed to. The Maplethorpes were a powerful family. Their son was a war hero. When they said it was an accident, we couldn't argue. We moved away. We had to."

You left me.

"I felt so bad. But Ruthie was already dead. She couldn't be hurt anymore."

Everybody thinks the dead have no feelings. They're wrong. The dead are nothing but feelings. They have no bodies to be comforted.

"She is hurt," Hannah said.

"Could you tell her I'm sorry?" Mildred said.

What good is being sorry?

"You can tell her. She's listening," Hannah said.

No, I wasn't. What was the point? It wouldn't change anything.

"I'm sorry for what I said," Mildred said.

"What did you say?" Hannah said.

"I was over there with the Andrews boy." She pointed with her cane to the far side of the pond. "We came out here to get away from her. She had already cut up all my dresses, including the one I was going to wear to the dance that night. And she came sneaking around the other side of the pond. Spying on us."

You told the soldier I was there. You said, "Enemy approaching."

"You called her the enemy," Hannah said.

"No, no. *He* was the enemy. I was trying to warn Ruth about him."

She was lying.

"He was sneaking up on her. He had this stick he thought was a gun. He hit her in the head. She fell into the pond. Right about where that red tree is."

Everybody looked at the tree.

"I ran around the pond as fast as I could. I waded out to her. Her hands were clutching the weeds. I couldn't pull her up. I was too late to save her."

Hannah put her arms around Anna.

"If only Father had let us learn how to swim," Mildred said.

I didn't say anything. There was nothing to say.

"Ruthie? Can you hear me? I'm so sorry. Can you know that? I'm sure you hated me all these years. Maybe now you won't quite so much."

Tears streamed down her face again. I knew how terrible she had felt all these years. I knew she had suffered too.

Emily got out the handkerchief. It was still wet from the last round of tears. When Mildred tried to wipe her face, it just smeared the tears around. So I blew gently at my sister's cheeks.

When she realized what I was doing, she cried even harder.

Then I blew her skirt up again. I didn't want to hang around all day drying tears.

There had been enough crying.

31

They didn't leave right away. Lydia wanted to see the writing on the closet door. Mildred had to use the bathroom. Everybody sat on the porch steps.

Now Mildred was eager to tell all kinds of stories. Her memory wasn't very accurate. She said I had cracked the hall tree mirror, when she was the one who threw her hairbrush at me. Did she think it was my fault because I ducked?

"Ruthie always had her nose in a book. Usually this one." Mildred was holding my copy of *The Story of the Treasure Seekers*.

"I want to get her a new copy," Hannah said.

"One with all the pages," Anna said.

They were trying to be nice. They knew they would all be leaving soon. And I wouldn't.

It was sad. But I didn't blame Mildred anymore for

what had happened to me. I was glad she had lived long enough for me to see her again. I still didn't care that much for Emily, but I liked meeting Lydia. She looked more than a little bit like me. I could tell Mildred thought so too.

I went to my sister. I thought as hard as I could. *I'm sorry I hated you.*

Mildred clapped her hands. "You know, I think I heard her that time."

"What did she say? I want to hear her again," Lydia said.

"It's a secret between me and my sister." Mildred turned to Hannah. "Do I have to answer out loud?"

"No. She reads your thoughts," Hannah said.

Just like we do, Anna thought.

Hannah smiled. She was also glad to have her sister back.

Mildred thought how much she had missed me all these years.

And I was happy.

Suddenly I understood why I had been unable to leave. I would have gone to her with anger. And caused more and more hate.

That wasn't the only bad thing I had done.

Anna and Hannah sat side by side on the steps. They looked like twins again, even though Hannah was a little pale and Anna's hair still had all those braids. It had been very wrong of me to try to come between them. It had been dangerous too.

Luckily Anna had been able to listen to me. She

had saved her sister. And my sister had tried to save me. I knew that now.

I felt something get lighter in my heart.

I blew gently on my sister's cheek one last time.

Then I lifted up and soared away from the humans, away from the golden field, and far, far from the house on Hemlock Road.

I only looked back once, to see the red car drive off. Hannah and Anna stood with their arms around each other, waving.

Good-bye, good-bye. Thank you for helping me be free.

I hoped the twins could hear me. I was traveling such a vast distance. And yet I was certain they knew how happy I was. Just like with the story of the Bastables, everything had all come right in the end.

I soared on and on, through the day, into the night, and beyond the stars.

ACKNOWLEDGMENTS

This book wouldn't exist without the expert guidance of my editor, Shana Corey. I'm also grateful to my agent, Linda Pratt; my husband, Lee; and my daughter, Sofia, for their wonderful advice and support.

JANE KELLEY is the author of the middle-grade novel *Nature Girl*. She lives in Brooklyn, New York, with her husband, her daughter, and a black cat who sometimes cries in the night for no apparent reason. You can visit Jane's website at JaneKelleyBooks.com.